The Land of Dragons

and Dreams

(A young adult fantasy novel)

K.S. Riggin

Table of Contents

Prelude 1

Chapter One: The Beginning 2

Chapter Two 15

Chapter Three 21

Chapter Four 33

Chapter Five.. 38

Chapter Six 42

Chapter Seven 52

Chapter Eight 57

Chapter Nine 66

Chapter Ten... 73

Chapter Eleven.. 79

Chapter Twelve.. 89

Chapter Thirteen 93

Chapter Fourteen.. 99

Chapter Fifteen 105

Chapter Sixteen... 108

Chapter Seventeen 111

Chapter Eighteen.. 115

Chapter Nineteen 119

Chapter Twenty.. 123

Chapter Twenty-One.. 128

Chapter Twenty-Two.. 132

Chapter Twenty-Three 141

Chapter Twenty-Four 147

Chapter Twenty-Five 152

Chapter Twenty-Six 158

Chapter Twenty-Seven 172

Chapter Twenty-Eight 178

Chapter Twenty-Nine 189

Chapter Thirty 195

Prelude

A crash, an abduction, and an entirely new world,

a world with magic and dragons.

Different species in hues of blues.

Kings and queens and beautiful princesses.

Is it a better world or a worse one?

I don't know.

Perhaps it's a choice that everyone must make,

everyone who is chosen by the Wizard,

but magic and love live there.

For me, that made all the difference.

Chapter One
The Beginning

You've found my book, but don't be surprised if it isn't what you wanted to read. I didn't plan it this way, but when you throw down pick-up-sticks, sometimes they land in a heap of tangled colors so dense you can't separate them. What happened to me looked like that — a heap of tangled colors with a mound of sharp, prickly points.

I thought I was normal, set to graduate from Pinecrest Academy, a small, rather prestigious boarding school where parents sent kids when they didn't want to bother with them. I'd done okay in academics — not brilliant or anything, but mostly B's, a sprinkling of A's. Chatsworth University accepted me, no great surprise since it's my Dad's alma mater. Things looked good until the day my life soured even worse than usual.

Graduation day, a hot, muggy June afternoon. Picture it. In the courtyard, all the seats were taken except two, the ones saved for my parents. They'd purchased the seats and reserved them for themselves. Front row, too. Great seats for a show they were about to miss.

Thirty-five graduating seniors, a ceremony scheduled to last three hours because each of us needed to give a speech. It was our *civic duty*, our final grade for public speaking class. I'd practiced mine over and over, timed it precisely, the minimum length. With my parents absent and derelict in their duty, I figured no one would care whether or not I elaborated on my future plans. I cut out half. Besides, I was ticked off, fuming because my attorney parents hadn't shown up.

I felt sick, too, the excuse I planned to use with my speech teacher. Nausea kept me from eating breakfast. Betrayal rubbed vinegar against my insides.

Why? I should have been used to it. My parents rarely came to functions. Not mine, anyway.

With my speech finished, brief but sweet, I sat down. I'm sure everyone was relieved; one less speech to endure. A spatter of applause, next name called.

The sun hammered us; the tent provided little shade. Lights strung across the top poles made the graduates look like circus performers. The heat they gave off didn't help either, but the girls oohed and aahed over the effect. The first lesson to adulthood. Appearance counts more than any deed.

Electric fans blew a steady spew of hot air, directed at the other side, of course. We students smoldered in heavy caps and gowns. I wiggled in my seat, trying to get more comfortable, shot a glance behind, out in the parking lot, searching for late arrivals. No incoming.

Metal against cloth-covered buns. The guests had padded seats. Paying customers receive better service. That was rule number two on the way the world works.

Thirteen speeches followed mine, and I had lots of time to wonder why my parents hadn't bothered to attend. They hadn't forgotten. They called me the night before and even volunteered to take me to *Chez Louis*, a restaurant I'd wanted to try for four years.

I guess their failure to arrive should have been expected. My folks never had time for me. Rule number three: Paying customers are always worth more. More time. More attention. More of everything.

My parents believed in quick visits: "How are you, son? I saw you got an "A" in French and in Advanced Mathematics. Good job. But a

"C" in English? We need to talk. No "C's" on your record. I spoke to the dean. Write a term paper on Franklin D. Roosevelt. The dean says he'll change the grade to a "B." All right, son?"

"Sure, Dad."

"Well." Picture a quick glance down at his expensive watch. "Sorry, short visit this time, meeting a client. Everything else okay?"

I nod.

"Just as well," he grins. "You have work to do, don't you? Roosevelt, Franklin D."

We shake hands. I walk my father out. I head for the library.

Repeat the scene two or three times a year. Got it?

Whenever my folks felt guilty, they lectured me about something. Rule Four was Thrust and Parry. I know all about that. I guess, in layman's terms, that's block and evade. (Or attack before someone rises up to defend themselves.)

I was the school's top contender in fencing. Dad ended it.

"Not useful," he said, switching me into wrestling. I learned that sport, too, karate, equitation, cross country jumping. I took them all, but I didn't excel. What's the point? My father claimed that I needed to be well-rounded, so he moved me each time I got good.

I'm a wimp, you see, a wimp who can't stand up to my father, but debating an expert is not a challenge. It's stupidity. My father was an expert. Of course, he was. He was an attorney. They get paid to argue.

I could have told Dad why the teacher gave me the "C," but there wasn't time. Dad wouldn't have listened anyway. Maybe I could have argued more for the fencing competition. I wanted to go to State. The school needed me, too. That would have been something, something great.

But I didn't argue. I didn't tell my mom, either. No point. She always backed Dad, even when she saw my side or said she did.

Besides, what difference did it make? Another term paper. Another sport. No big deal. Ideals, dreams of glory. Who needs them?

Sometimes, I couldn't help my thoughts, though. I plotted out what I should have said. "Dad, I got a "C" cause I wrote about public schools being better for the nation than private ones. Excellent paper, Dad. You should read it. It didn't deserve a D."

"Public schools?" Dad would have gasped as if I'd said we should toss out the legal systems and become barbarians. I could almost see his nose wrinkling up as if someone had given him a hors d'oeuvre with too much salt. "Why would you write about that? You've never been to a public school."

Of course, Dad had never committed a crime either, but he represented clients who had. I suppose it was just as well I didn't make my case. He would have summarized the situation with an offhand, "Give the teacher what he wants. Get an "A," and move forward. Nothing complicated, Benjamin. It's only high school, remember?"

As I said, it didn't matter. He and Mom would drive off after their quick visit, waving once, leaving me a fifty dollar bill or a hundred if they were feeling guiltier than usual. Bills like that seemed to grow in Dad's wallet. He never missed them and never noticed their passage.

I once asked him for five hundred dollars, telling him I needed new skis. He handed the amount to me without a word, fresh new bills — five of them. He never asked on his next visit if I'd enjoyed skiing. Good thing. I didn't buy the skis. I didn't go.

But on the day of graduation, the rite of independence for every kid, just like always, my parents let me down.

Damn, I know I sound like a spoiled brat. I'm a really lucky kid. I know that. But all of my peers were advantaged kids with years of privilege, and yet, the look in their parents' eyes said it all. These parents were happy with their brats. Every one of the mothers and fathers was proud of his child that day.

Wasn't this the chance to boast and swagger around because their kid had achieved a diploma? Their darling child had more or less made it into adulthood. Well, maybe not all the way. College followed. But it was a step in that direction. An accomplishment.

My thoughts had turned sour and immature. Sorry about that. But the exciting part comes soon. The part where the mystery happens …

The graduation ceremony went on and on. I wiped the sweat off my brow using an initial-engraved white handkerchief. That made me think about my mother. The hankies formed her major contribution to my existence, well, other than giving birth. She handed hankies to everyone, embroidered in her spare time. She sewed fancy stitches in between cases or while waiting for a client.

Every month, she sent me a package with elegant B's for Benjamin. My drawers were filled with them. I had twenty-three different colors of initials. The kerchiefs smelled nice, at least for a while, not that she scented them. They smelled like her. I raised one to my nose and breathed it in.

Last speech. Evan, next to me, groaned. "Here comes the longest one."

Donald, the kid at the podium, wanted to be a lawyer. He would debate anyone. He could take either side of any argument. Most of us figured he invented facts when he didn't have the data, but we couldn't prove it. We could never catch him when he couldn't name his source. So, maybe he was a genius with a brain that held onto stuff like that.

But it got old. No one would debate him *or* listen to him. If he ever became an attorney and made it into court, he'd win the case just because he'd bored the jury and judge to death. They'd fall over in a faint, break down and sob, or worse. The headline would say: *Tedium kills. Another win for Donald.*

Donald was in full battle that day with an audience of captives. His eyes scanned the audience, checked for conflict, searched for … who knew what. Maybe he was wondering if he needed to wake them up before speaking. Probably no one was listening, except maybe Donald's folks. I turned my head to search for them, but I didn't see anyone beaming at his brilliance.

"Sit still," Evan said.

I turned back around.

I yawned and watched Donald hug the podium. The heat and my parent's betrayal sapped my energy. My stomach gurgled a low-pitched song. I sagged further down in my chair.

I used the engraved hankie to wipe my face and tried not to hear the whispers behind me mocking my noisy stomach. Amid the shifts of creaky chairs and the drone of Donald talking on and on, I wondered if that killing boredom I'd envisioned was about to strike me down.

The cops arrived during Donald's speech. No sirens. Just lights, the circulating blue kind that sits atop their vehicles. A dry wind kept flapping the corners of the tent, creating a light show for those not watching the speaker.

Whispers grew louder than Donald's voice. At last, he wrapped up his speech and stomped off to his seat in a row somewhere behind me. A few people clapped. The noise level grew.

Why would the police come to Pinecrest Academy? I could feel the interest rising. People were waking up and coming alive.

"Four cop cars," Joe whispered after peeking through the crack.

"Some kid's done a high school prank. Wonder what it was," Mary Ann said in a loud stage whisper.

We snickered, though none of us was a prankster. The idea was breathtaking. Pinecrest Academy trained students in civility. Hadn't we been lectured about it for the past four years? Besides, not even Stephen Jibs, the class clown, could think up a prank notable enough to call out that many cops.

The officers didn't interfere with the chancellor's speech, which came next. They just sat there in their cars, waiting. What were they pausing for? Why didn't they interrupt and barge in? It would have been worth it to see. The chancellor's face would turn beet red. His forehead had a bulge that throbbed strangely when he got upset. It did pushups on his forehead.

But it didn't matter. We weren't watching him. He'd lost our attention before he stood behind the podium. We were too tuned into the scene outside, taking peeks through the tent cracks and whispering, *Why are they here?*

"Maybe they're here for the chancellor," someone whispered.

Oh, no. He was looking our way. We shuffled back to sitting erect, head to the front, eyes on the chancellor, faces demonstrating fascination. All that training had turned us into model students. Except, what we'd best learned was how to fake it.

I bet not one of us could repeat a single word of the chancellor's speech — not even the topic of it, although it's a good bet it was the usual — our role in society.

In the end, when the chancellor had finally run down, we threw our caps in the air. A moment later, I heard doors slam, the tramp of heavy-soled shoes. Four officers made their way toward us — three men and one woman. The female stood as tall as the men. She walked with a military tread, in shoes flat and ugly as boots. The G-men, if that's what they were, wore shirts that bulged at the arms, eyes on alert.

All around me, kids kept hugging and kissing. Their families took pictures, wept, smiled, and laughed. I scuffed my right shoe, kicked at one of the metal chairs, and reminded myself for the umpteenth time that my parents' betrayal didn't matter. Then I eyed the cops' approach.

"Are you Benjamin Thorne?" one of the cops asked. The question startled me. I slid sideways and almost fell.

Seeing the cops gave me a bad taste in my mouth — the jitters, I guess you might say. But I had nothing to feel guilty about. I'd never done anything wrong — never stolen a pack of gum or a candy bar, never broken into a deserted house, or tried to buy liquor without a driver's license. To say I walked the straight and narrow was a good way to put it. If your father was the city attorney and your mother the chief district attorney, I guarantee you'd be lily clean, too.

But the shock of seeing these cops or G-men in front of me, having them ask me a question, showered me with guilt. I tried to get my mouth to curl around a "Yes, that's my name" when Sharon Doister — long, blonde-haired, deliciously formed Sharon Doister — broke away from her parents to interfere in my business.

"What seems to be the problem, officer?" she said.

The middle-aged policeman bobbed his Adam's apple, just like the rest of us guys did whenever Sharon Doister came near. He stuttered, too. "Uh, I was just . . . uh, uh…"

The woman officer pushed him aside. "We're trying to locate Benjamin Thorne. Are you he?" she said, giving the man beside her a stern look and a shake of her head.

I felt sure the female cop could peer into someone's soul and pull out his worst, deep, dark secret. I gulped and spit out, "Yes, ma'am." Of course, my voice went from male to female soprano in the second part of ma'am.

My stomach churned at a higher rate. I felt ill.

"What do you want with him?" Sharon Doister interrupted a second time, her chest swelling out with indignation.

I licked my lips, then looked away. Sharon's body brought about most of my nightly fantasies. I was glad she was standing so close, yet . . .

Waves of nausea swept through me. I needed to lie down, but I didn't dare ask if I could. Did they have cots in the local jail?

"Of course, he's Benjamin Thorne," Sharon said. "Everyone knows Benjamin. He was our fencing champion three years running."

Parts of me came alive at that moment. I looked down and counted pebbles on the fancy sidewalk — seven browns, nine grays.

I felt the officers' eyes on me — heck — probably the whole school was watching.

With my already scuffed right shoe, I kicked at one of the pebbles. It was locked in place. Again, I almost tripped. Sharon Doister caught my elbow. Her grip pinched. I felt grateful for the pain.

The female cop studied me, her eyes the exact color of dirty, rusted pennies. She moved on to scan Sharon. Sharon had three snaps of her graduation robe undone and open. It showed a dress the color of lake water. I swallowed hard. The dress made Sharon's dark blue eyes even bluer. The sweetness of her perfume and those eyes drowned me.

"Benjamin," the female cop said, then ground to a halt. She cleared her throat. It drew my eyes from Sharon Doister, but only for a moment. Rusted pennies can't compare with ocean bliss.

"Benjamin," she tried again. Her copper pennies turned liquid. I watched them, wondering why.

I wet my lips in case the cop expected me to say something, but I had no idea what that would be. Nothing the police could say could ever compete with Sharon Doister's fragrance. I breathed in deeply, swaying from the pleasure of it, from my dizziness.

"I'm sorry to tell you this, Benjamin, but . . . there's been . . . an accident."

My heart stopped. I didn't drive. How could the police blame me for it?

The officer gazed at me, waiting for something. I forgot about Susan. My eyes locked on the copper pennies, trying to understand. I opened my mouth to explain I didn't have a driver's license, but everyone was staring. Sharon Doister's eyes had teared up. A dainty droplet lay glittering on her right cheek. I wanted to reach out and touch it . . .

I shook my head; the silence around me felt like a vacuum. Where had all the sound gone? Why weren't people breathing? Why were they staring at me as if they wanted me to do something, to react, to . . .?

"An accident?" I said. "Where?" I blinked my thoughts. "Who?"

Sharon stepped closer. She grabbed my hand and squeezed it. "Exactly what are you saying?" Sharon demanded.

With my other hand, I clutched the chair back. Someone turned the police car's blue light show off. I watched the tent flip back and forth. Now, only yellow light, the light from sunshine, played with the shadow.

"Your parents' car ran into a tree," the cop said. "I'm so sorry, Benjamin."

My eyes couldn't focus. The light shimmered, streaks darting back and forth as if being chased.

A tree? No! She was wrong. My parents wouldn't run into a tree. Not them. It's a mistake. My parents didn't do things like that. Never.

"Where are they?" I said. I pictured how angry my father would be. He was too important. He'd be furious if a tree got in his way.

The buzz grew louder, an echo chamber, everyone curling words around and around a narrow tube.

My parents? An accident? A tree? What was the officer saying? Had someone stolen my parents' vehicle? Is that why they hadn't come to my graduation?

"A tree?"

The woman shifted. Her navy blue uniform moved with her, something I shouldn't have noticed. She had a tiny waist. Her nylons made her legs glimmer. She was a cop. Why did I find myself staring at the crack of her slightly open blouse?

She felt my eyes. Her fingers reached up, tugged at the opening, and held it closed.

"We don't really know, Benjamin," she said. "Their car was destroyed, but . . ." She eyed me strangely. Because I'd looked down her blouse?

12

"Are they all right?" Sharon interrupted, changing the direction of my thoughts.

The woman's face grimaced.

I turned to look at the other officers.

The one overwhelmed by Sharon stepped forward. "We don't know exactly where they are, Benjamin. The car was destroyed, but your parents weren't in it. We don't know where. . ."

"What?" I sagged down into the nearest chair. The room was spinning like the police lights going around and around. I clutched the chair in front of me. Sharon's fragrance assaulted me. Penny's eyes watered. The crack in the woman's blouse had opened again.

I wiped my face with my right hand. Sweat drips.

The female turned a chair around and sat down like a woman riding a horse. My face heated. Sharon plopped down on the other side and wrapped her sweet little hand in mine. I groaned.

"Are you saying someone stole his parents' car?" Sharon said.

That is a good question. I looked up. The subject panged about in my head, but I couldn't eject it. The smells, the confusion, the overhead lights, the crowd of parents, the caps and gowns lying on the stage, my absent parents, all swimming, whirling like cop lights. What was wrong with me? Where were my parents? There was an accident. My parents' car?

The policewoman answered Sharon, but her eyes remained on me. "We don't know," she said. "We found these in the car. Are they your mother's?"

My eyes took in the handkerchiefs draped over the woman's hand, handkerchiefs with the initials BJ. Benjamin James Thorne. The embroidery was my mom's work. I nodded.

"We found a bag full of embroidery needles, thread, and blank handkerchiefs. Your mother's purse was there, too, but I'm afraid it was mangled rather badly. Her things were sprawled all over the . . ."

Tears sprang into my eyes, turning them into stinging orbs of pain. I wiped with my spare hand and stared at the pebbles again, unconsciously counting the grays.

"Is this necessary?" Sharon interrupted. "Can't you see he's going into shock?"

I blinked. Shock? Was that what it was? My brain was empty. My stomach was ready to heave. I felt icy cold and yet hot as the fires of Hell. The hand being held inside Sharon's warm one had gone numb.

"Maybe he should lie down," an unknown woman suggested.

I looked up to see who it was. I should have realized Sharon's mother would be standing there. Sharon introduced me. I stood and stretched out my hand to shake hers. That's all I remember. When I woke I was in the Medical Unit, the name given to the hospital ward of Pinecrest Academy.

Chapter Two

The first thing I saw when I came out of my faint was the poster about brushing your teeth. We'd each been given our own private copy and were supposed to have hung it up on our dorm room wall. Fat chance. Who needed a drawing of a rabbit showing buckteeth and a huge orange toothbrush? Most of us had other ideas about decorating our rooms.

It was obvious the poster was a favorite of the school's nurse, but it was not a pleasant thing to wake up to. I lay for several minutes wishing they had something else to study. My head was killing me. I didn't dare move it.

I don't know how long I was in that stunned state, but eventually I heard voices on the outside of the room. Stupidly, I called out. "Anyone there?"

Sharon came running in. She'd gotten rid of her graduation robe and was wearing a very tight and short, saucy, little blue dress. It was an absolute sigh of perfection. The toothbrush rabbit was instantly erased from my mind.

Sharon's beautiful body was elegantly displayed. The neck of the dress had a small opening, not nearly low enough, but still enticing. I swallowed hard and worked my way up to her face. She had tears in her eyes — tears for me!

Her mother and the officers followed her into the room. So did the white-smocked school nurse, Mrs. Jaybottoms. The latter had a thermometer in her hand and was shaking it. Mrs. Jaybottoms pushed forward, sliding in front of the glorious Sharon. I sighed heavily just as the woman slipped the thermometer into my mouth.

No one uses that kind of thermometer anymore. I wanted to tell her to go digital, but this kind of thermometer required minutes to wait for a temperature to register. Minutes of lying there with the thing under my tongue so I couldn't move, couldn't speak, couldn't do anything but hold the stupid thing in place.

I hadn't had time to ask a single question before it was shoved under my tongue. My brain was swimming with them. Or rather, questions were churning about my mind, all half-formed and heavy like the contents of a cement truck's rotating belly.

In the outside world they no longer used oral thermometers. I discovered that when I went to get a physical for Chatsworth University. In the doctor's office, they held a small device to my ear. Only at Pinecrest had progress stopped.

Besides, just because my parents had — what disappeared, vanished . . . Why in the world did I need my temperature taken? I wasn't the one doing the magic disappearing act the cop had talked about. But that was typical of Pinecrest Academy. I wondered if the nurse would insist I stand up and get on the scale. That was usually what came after a temperature reading.

"He's not sick," Sharon said, removing the thermometer and handing it back to the nurse. "He's in shock. He was just told that his parents…" She stopped and glanced at the police, but they didn't seem inclined to finish her sentence.

I decided at that moment, with Sharon once more taking the lead as if this were a play she'd wiggled herself into and grabbed the starring role, that I'd played the weakling too long. I sat up — a bit gradually and carefully since the lump on the left side of my skull felt like someone had attached a second head. My brain was still pounding, and the cement mixer inside my belly was churning around and around, but I was a man, wasn't I? (Not that my father would have called me that if he were here. Where was he?)

I guess while I was pondering that, my hand was massaging the huge lump that shouldn't be there.

"Oh, does your head hurt?" Susan's mother asked worriedly.

I started to nod but thought better of it. "Yes, ma'am. Is there an ice pack?" I asked.

The nurse nodded and left, still holding the rejected thermometer. I stared after her, surprised she hadn't argued about the temperature-taking process. Did Sharon really have that kind of power? Or was it the presence of an adult — a tuition-paying adult that had made the difference? Or maybe it was the existence of the cops in the room that had turned the normally argumentative Mrs. Jaybottoms into a silent vaudeville actor.

I glanced at the policewoman. There were more important items to think about than Mrs. Jaybottoms and the beautiful Sharon. I snagged a churning thought, sent it down into the mouth region, and spit it out. "You said my parents weren't in the car. Were they thrown out of it?"

The nurse rushed back to my side. Apparently, she'd regained some of her authority because she slapped the ice on my head so hard I rocked from the sound of it. The echo, as if it were coming down a long hall, thundered with pronounced regularity.

"Careful," Susan said. It felt like the nurse had attacked me, but I wasn't sure of anything anymore. The room was doing summersaults.

"I think he's got a concussion," Susan's mother said as she studied my eyes.

"Nonsense," said the nurse. "Let me see." She clamped her hands on my chin and rotated my head as if she were a dentist getting ready to yank out a tooth. I closed my eyes, unable to focus on anything but the wart below her lip and the fact that the room was turning into a gyrating washing machine.

I forced my mind back into focus. The nurse was peering down at me, pointing a small flashlight into my eyes. I blinked, then closed them. The woman's wart was making me even sicker.

"I'll be fine in a minute," I protested faintly. "Just explain, please." I took a breath, a long one, one that was supposed to take away my nausea. It didn't.

"What happened to my parents?" I blurted out, rushing through the words as if that were the only way I could get them out without spilling the gyrating juices inside me.

"Hold still, young man. This could be serious," the nurse demanded of me, and the vice-like hand securing my head squeezed tightly.

She shouldn't have done that. My stomach had been queasy even before I'd fainted. But it was inevitable then. My eruption shot out of me like the pictures I'd seen of Old Faithful — one mighty burst of noxious acid and a stench so putrid it more or less instantly cleared everyone out of the room.

I didn't dare look toward the door they'd used to exit. Hearing their rush out was enough to inform me that I'd gone from being the object of their concern to being the most unpopular guy in Pinecrest Academy.

I lay back, feeling even worse, wondering if Sharon would ever speak to me again.

No one reentered the room. Even the nurse left me alone.

The smell of my discharge at first nauseated me, but after a few minutes, in the silence of the people-emptied room, the smell either faded or I became immune to it. With my eyes still closed, I listened for sounds of the crowd — okay, for Sharon's voice. The memory of her in that sweet blue dress was like clean, clear water. I could breathe it in, taste it, smell its deliciousness.

Maybe I was hallucinating. I heard bells. For a second, I thought I was dying and being called into heaven, but I was pretty sure that wasn't true. I'd never done anything to deserve heaven. And besides, my life was just starting. It was my parents who . . .

I sat up sharply. Nausea hit me again. I threw a hand over my mouth, wanting to halt a second explosion, but I knew that if there'd been another geyser formulating, that wouldn't have stopped it.

The bells were growing louder. Alarms? A fire drill? Surely the school wouldn't expect me to get off the sick room bed and trudge out into the courtyard while they made the fire department happy? But it wasn't a fire alarm. It was an ambulance. I heard someone yelling, "He's in here."

Was it me they were talking about? The sound of hard-leather boot soles tramping across the old-fashioned wooden floor gave me little doubt. By the time they reached me, I was expecting them, but I still wasn't prepared for the gurney and all the emergency equipment they brought in with them. One medic slammed his box of goodies onto the top of the sickroom cabinet. Two bandages slid to the floor.

"What's the problem?" the paramedic asked, his eyes raking over the vomit on the floor. "Been drinking?"

I started to shake my head, but even the thought of that sent up another gusher.

"We've got us one sick puppy," the guy told the others.

"Bet he was drinking," said one of the gurney holders.

"I don't drink," I managed to get out before nausea hit me again.

"You mean it's just the flu?" the third guy piped in, looking at me like I'd wasted their time.

"I don't think so. My parents… they're . . ." I didn't know what to say. Should I say they were missing? Had they been kidnapped? Was there a ransom? Why hadn't the police explained better?

"Ask the police, please."

"Blood pressure's a bit fast for a kid his age. Do you take anything? Pills? Dope?"

I knew not to move. "I don't drink, and I don't do drugs," I told him, eyeing the needle he was about to poke into my arm.

"Ouch!" I winced. "What's that for?"

"Okay, he's stabilized. Let's take him," the first paramedic said.

I wasn't ready when they swung me onto the gurney. I hadn't even understood they were going to move me. I should have known. If I'd been thinking clearly, I would have, but my brain had gone numb. Everything was distorted as if I were swimming underwater, or more likely, in mud.

I closed my eyes as they carried me forward. The rabbit with the toothbrush was the last thing I saw at Pinecrest Academy. I passed out again somewhere in the hallway. I didn't even get another look at Sharon's cobalt blue graduation dress.

Chapter Three

I woke in the ambulance. There was a bag of water that I at first thought was flying through the air, but after a couple of blinks and a slow return to consciousness, I realized I was on my way to the hospital, and it was merely a bladder full of liquid waving like a wind-tossed flag. In the next instant, when I tried to scratch my itchy hand, I discovered I was tied to that bag.

"What?" I cried out, my voice sounding tiny and weak.

The man beside me, the one pushing my hand away from the connecting cord, had a badge on his jacket that proclaimed him to be *Charles*.

"What's going on?" I whispered. "Where are my folks?"

"It's going to be okay," the guy said, grabbing my wrist and placing it back on my stomach.

The ambulance wasn't using a siren, but it was rocking from side to side as if speeding down the main thoroughfare.

"I don't need to go to the hospital," I said.

"Don't worry. That fancy school of yours is paying for it," said the other medic. His uniform said *Philip* across the pocket.

The medics were missing the point. I hadn't even thought about money. I started to explain all that had happened when Charles place a thermometer on my ear.

Now I know that logically, I can speak and have my temperature taken at the same time, but I lost my train of thought. I waited for Charles to remove it before trying to argue my case.

"It's normal, isn't it?" I demanded.

Charles was staring at it, trying to read the numbers. He glanced over at me, then shook his head. "Not unless you always run a temperature of 102."

Up until that time, I'd been fine, but with his words, I suddenly noticed the sweat on my face. My body felt clammy. My throat hurt. Someone seemed to be sitting on my chest.

I opened my mouth, but I didn't want to say anything. Somehow, I slid back into twilight consciousness and remained silent for the rest of the trip.

At the hospital, they scanned my brain and gave me several tests. The result of it all was exactly as Susan's mother had suggested. I had a concussion in addition to a touch of flu. Hooked up to the intravenous bag and lying in clean, white sheets wasn't so bad after all. I slept the rest of the day, not even waking when various nurses stopped by to check what they called my "vitals."

When I finally came back to earth more fully, I discovered that I was lying in a room full of flowers. Susan and her mother had sent me a bouquet of daisies and something orange and exotic, accompanied by a note saying how sorry they were they couldn't come to visit me since they had to catch a flight to Paris that evening.

So much for any interest I might have attached to Susan's concern for me. The touch of her hand on my arm had almost scorched me. The way she'd looked in her blue dress . . . I sighed. I shouldn't be thinking about girls anyway. Where were my parents? Why weren't they at the hospital?

A middle-aged woman, one who looked very much like the Pinecrest Academy's chief math teacher, fed me dinner — one red gelatin. It was all I could keep down — and for a while, that was even questionable. Yet I survived the night with no more volcano-like eruptions. Hospitals are not good places to sleep, but despite that, morning came before I was ready for it.

At five a.m., a nurse decided to give me a sponge bath even though my eyes were only half-mast. She was younger than the previous nurse. She had blonde hair, too, but in spite of her being nice to look at, her manner was that of a drill sergeant, and I was very uncomfortable with what she was doing. Then, as if that weren't bad enough, I needed to urinate, and she expected me to do it while she was standing there — right into a small, pink-colored jar.

To say that Janet and I didn't hit it off is an exaggeration of the day. When she finally let me go back to sleep, I was exhausted. But I was clean, and my urgent need for the bathroom had at least been taken care of.

Later in the morning, at a more reasonable time, I came awake enough to be hit by the stench of more flower bouquets, ones that had miraculously appeared while I was sleeping. A nurse read the note from Pinecrest Academy which, although it said it was sorry for my illness and for the tragedy of my parents' loss, informed me — rather coldly, I thought — *that they were not to blame for anything, and since I'd already graduated and was no longer a student at the Academy, were not responsible for any future hospital expenses.* The note ended with: *We wish you well, Bentley.*

Lovely. They didn't even get my name right.

I asked the nurse to donate the flowers to someone else. I couldn't bear the smell of them or the chill of their reminder that I apparently had no one who gave a darn.

For the rest of the day, I lay in the clean white bed inside a white-walled private room with one shuttered window. I thought about my situation. Of course, I puzzled over my parents, wondering if they were dead, missing them, worrying, mourning their probable deaths, but then I began to feel sorry for myself. I wept a bit, moaned because of my aching head, and slept.

In the late afternoon, after a lunch of the same red gelatin and three soda crackers, the female cop came around. I was actually glad to see her.

"How are you, Benjamin?" she asked.

At least she had my name right. My head was still throbbing. My throat felt like someone had ripped part of it out, my body ached, and I was, in general, feeling the most miserable of my whole short-lived life, but I told her I was better. That was apparently the appropriate thing to say.

She sat down on the chair beside my bed, pulled out a pad and a pencil, and said, "We haven't found out any more about your parents. Have they contacted you?"

I still didn't dare attempt a head shake. My brain felt barely attached to the rest of me, with only the pain portion remaining. I gave the cop a grave, raspy "no" and reached up to grab the pink plastic glass of water sitting on the wheeled table stretched across my bed. I sipped through the straw, then returned the cup. The water was tepid. I could barely swallow it. The exertion of energy that the process required completely exhausted me. I lay back against the pillow and panted.

I could feel the woman watching me. Her gaze felt intensely hot. I think she waited a moment for my breathing to calm down or maybe to see my eyes open again.

When they did, I didn't look at her. I stared at the water glass, wishing I had the energy to take another drink.

"We are still investigating the case," the cop said solemnly.

I glanced at her and saw her eyes studying me as if she suspected I knew more than I was telling her. Again, she fell silent. I closed my eyes and thought about what I should be asking her.

"Need anything?" she asked me, but her eyes were scanning the room as if expecting to find a clue that might give her the answer.

"Well…" I started to say, but I was too drowsy to go on. My lips were having trouble making words, and my head, the one that was hardly there, was weighing down my body. I don't remember if I finished my sentence. I can't remember even what I was going to ask for.

I think she was my only visitor, the only one I remember, anyway. I missed seeing my friends, but most of the guys I hung around with had headed out after graduation, bound for someplace exotic — either because they were whooping it up in Europe or because they'd signed up for a last trip with their parents before college.

A few days later, the doctor came in while I was watching a rerun of *I Love Lucy*. I'd just eaten a turkey sandwich and some of the ever-present red gelatin. My headache was almost gone, and I'd even been up and around a couple of times, probably driving the nurses crazy with my demands for them to call the police station so I could find out what had happened to my parents.

The doctor checked my chart, took my pulse, and said, "We're releasing you, Benjamin. You're doing much better."

That was great news. I was tired of being locked up in a sterile hospital cell. I thanked the doctor, listened to his sermon about the things I needed to do to keep my headaches from coming back, and accepted the papers he handed me that had everything all written out and documented.

It was afternoon, but I was still in one of their ever-present open-backed hospital nightgowns. I asked a passing nurse about my clothes. She gestured at the wooden panel on the right and then left to check that the rest of my paperwork was ready for my departure.

I was still a bit shaky on my legs, but by holding onto the bed and then the wall, I made my way to the place she'd indicated. Truthfully, I hadn't realized the room even had a closet, but then I hadn't spent a lot of time awake. I found my clothes inside a panel that opened when I pressed against it. My suit was clean and ironed. I grabbed it off the hangar and dressed as quickly as possible, nervous that a nurse might return before I was fully ready. Of course, I wished I had a pair of jeans instead of a suit, but beggars can't be choosers. Anything was an improvement over the open-back hospital gown.

The nurse soon returned with a wheelchair that she insisted I sit in. Then she pushed me down the long, bare halls and into the elevator for the trip down to the lobby. As I felt the downward plunge that came from dropping several floors, it occurred to me that I had no way to get home. Should I call a taxi? Could I walk to the bus stop?

Of course, my parents had business partners. I could call one of them, I supposed. We had neighbors, too. The Gillicuttys were the elderly couple who lived next door. They'd always been good to me. In fact, I considered them the grandparents I'd never had. Unfortunately, the hospital was too far for them to drive, which is why I knew they hadn't come to see me.

They had sent a note with a cheerful bouquet of flowers — the non-stinky kind. I smiled, thinking about their card. Their words had meant a lot. I'd been feeling so alone. At least I had their friendship. It was nice to know someone still cared.

The hospital gave me back my wallet. I checked it over and signed the release form. I had a hundred dollar bill tucked down beneath one of the flaps, the emergency money that Dad always insisted I keep. In the fat part of the wallet were some ones and a couple of tens. How much would a cab cost?

I still had some paperwork to sign at the checkout station, forms like I'd already filled out before. All of them asked me the same things over and over. Luckily, I didn't owe anything. That was the good part. As the medic had said, the school had covered my stay.

When all the papers were filled out and I'd officially been discharged, I returned to the lobby and found the policewoman waiting for me there.

"I thought you might need a ride home," she said.

Home? The word stung. I wiped at a watering eye and nodded. "Thanks," I said. "I appreciate it."

I slipped into the black and white police car parked at the front of the hospital. I was nervous about sitting next to her. "Where's your partner?" I asked, and she smiled, but she didn't answer. She started up the car and pulled away from the curb.

At first I felt like a kid in grade school and had a mad desire to ask her to start up the siren. I squelched the request and instead made sure my seatbelt was secure, set the bag the hospital had given me on the floor, and watched as the woman drove quietly and sedately down the main boulevard.

It was a sunny day. The heat was jungle-damp, full of humidity and weight, but inside, once the car got moving, the air conditioner blew out the air so cold it chilled my fingers. It felt good. I cupped some, then touched my fingers to my face.

I was trying to wait for Detective Smith to talk, but I couldn't stand the silence. As we finally drifted out onto the main state highway, I burst out with a clump of questions. "What have you learned? What happened to my parents? How could a car be empty of drivers? Who was driving it? Did someone kidnap my parents?"

Detective Smith didn't look at me while I was quizzing her right and left. Her eyes remained focused straight ahead, like she was a brand new driver – or as if she didn't want to look me in the eye. I knew it was the latter. I took a breath and stopped babbling, attempting to simmer down my exasperation.

The seats of the car were grayish-blue leather. They reeked of cigarette smoke, although Detective Smith didn't smell like she smoked. I wondered if her partner did.

The dashboard matched the seats, but it had so many panels and keyboards and things that there was hardly space for anything else. I wondered if the car had a good sound system. Did cops ever play music? Were they allowed?

Detective Smith took a quiet breath, glanced at me and away, then answered. "We don't know, Benjamin. Your parents started out in their car. They stopped for gas at a station on the way. They were heading for Pinecrest for your graduation, as you know. But something happened. We don't understand what yet. They just disappeared. We're afraid they must have stopped to pick up a hitchhiker…"

I shook my head and laughed. "Dad? He'd never do that. Mom wouldn't either. They always lectured me about strangers. They'd never pick up a hitchhiker."

With a voice a degree louder than before and gruff, Detective Smith said, "Then you tell me what you think, Benjamin. Why would your parents start out on a drive and then just disappear? What else could explain it?"

I sighed and turned to stare out the window. How could I explain my parents to this woman? She wouldn't understand. Dad and Mom were just not like that. They'd never disappear. They were responsible people.

"What about their cell phones?" I asked. "Did you try to call their numbers?"

The detective nodded.

A voice suddenly shot out from the police radio, giving coded numbers. The cop gave me a look and turned it lower.

"Of course we did, Benjamin. Your parents' cells were out of range. No response. Wherever the phones were taken, it wasn't within a twenty-five mile radius of the car. And your parents couldn't have been nearby, Benjamin, or we would have found them."

I watched a semi-pass us on the right. Officer Smith was a slow driver. The semi was hauling lumber, stacks and stacks of it. The wood was pale and yellowish. I wondered where it would end up — a housing project, a church building, someone's tree house . . .

I sighed, letting out frustration and attempting to let out my anxiety over their disappearance. Did I mention, that I loved my parents? So, of course, I was worried about them.

"My parents would never leave their work behind. Surely they've checked in with their offices?" I said.

Officer Smith's hair was short and curly. When she shook her head, the curls jumped. "No. Your parents never canceled their appointments. Your mother had a big case on Monday. She didn't show up at the courthouse."

My head was hurting again. I rifled through my bag of things and pulled out the container of pain pills the doctor had sent with me. I popped a capsule into my mouth and washed it down with some bottled water the hospital had included in the bag.

"Headache again?" the detective asked, her eyes concerned.

I nodded. "They're not coming as often now or as bad, but I need to lie back and relax for a few minutes if you don't mind."

I think she nodded, but I'd closed my eyes to filter out the light coming in through the windowpane. I didn't mean to, but I fell asleep. I was doing that a lot. Sleeping through the days. It helped the headache, as well as offered me a chance to avoid thinking.

I didn't wake up until the car hit our gravel driveway. Somehow, I recognized the sound. It brought me up from a dream about my parents — one in which they were calling out to me from the mists surrounding an old castle. I was just about to reach out and touch my mother's hand when I heard the sound of the gravel.

Being jerked away from a dream like that flooded me with new disappointment. It was as if my parents had faded away again, even though I knew intellectually it was only a dream. But the dream had felt real, as had the sight of them, the smell, and the sound of my mother's voice.

I used my key on the front door. The house was cold. It felt unlived. As Detective Smith searched briefly for any signs of habitation, I started the kettle. I didn't feel like drinking tea, but it seemed the right thing to do. It's what my parents would have done.

The kitchen was immaculate. Only the fine layer of several days' accumulated dust lessened its perpetual shine. I reached up and took down two mugs. They were both hand-formed ceramics in the cobalt blue wash my mother found so attractive. I hunted for some milk, but of course, there was none usable. I poured the quart of lumps and sour smells down the sink, then rinsed it and tossed the container into the garbage can. I ran the garbage disposal and scrubbed the sink. Mother was always so fastidious about doing so. She hated the idea of things gone bad. Sour smells were a personal offense.

As I was straightening up, Detective Smith walked around the house, treading softly like a hunting cat. I was just reaching for the sugar and creamer when I felt her presence behind me. "A cup of tea?" I asked.

She shook her head. "I have to get back to work. Will you be okay here, Benjamin? Is there someone you can call?"

There was no one, but I didn't tell her that. I nodded my head and walked her to the door. "I'll be fine," I said. "Please just find my parents. Don't give up. Okay?"

For a moment, she looked like she was wavering about leaving me there. But the police had already discussed the situation with me. I was on the borderline between adulthood and adolescence. Theoretically, they'd admitted that I should be placed in a foster home, but I'd just graduated from high school. Even though I was only seventeen still, the judge had permitted me to remain at home, tentatively — on a trial basis until my parents showed up or . . .

I could tell that Detective Smith didn't think that wise. She looked like she was about to lecture me on wild parties or doing some of the other things most kids my age might plan. But I wasn't like other kids. I was my parents' child — a good student, well-behaved, mature, and diligent. (Although my father might have argued on the latter point. I was pretty sure he deemed me stuck in Lazyville.)

I could feel the stress in the cop. I think that's why, when she said goodbye, she avoided my eyes. I watched from the doorway as she headed out to the police car and slipped inside. Detective Smith, who must be at least thirty, had a very shapely rear. I sighed, mentally slapped myself for noticing, and closed the heavy door. Then I reentered the kitchen, poured myself a mug of hot water, and added a package of cocoa powder.

The day was sunny. I could hear birds singing, even through the tightly shut windows. I nibbled a couple of cookies from the canister where Dad always kept them. Then I put my feet up on a chair, drank my cocoa, and wondered once again where on earth my parents were.

Chapter Four

That night, I slept in my old bedroom. It felt strange. I hadn't used it in several years. My vacations from school had all been travel sessions meant to broaden my knowledge of the world, according to my father. I'd been to most of the countries in Europe and attended classes at various small colleges in classical music, art, French, Spanish, German, and Italian. In the States, I'd attended computer camps, space camps, soccer camps, and scuba diving camps on the main island of Hawaii. Last year I'd even gone down to Australia to "work" at a wild animal park for the summer. But I'd rarely spent time at home.

My bed felt wonderful — hard enough for good sleeping and without the lump on the right side that my dorm room's bed had possessed. Still, I tossed around a bit, played with the lighting, not wanting to face the dark alone, and then finally drifted off into a shallow, unrelaxing kind of twilight sleep. And I dreamed.

Dad was fishing in a moat. His pole was a branch of a tree. His line was from some kind of native grasses formed into a slender rope. When he brought out the end of it, I saw the hook, fashioned from one of Mother's earrings. Where was Mom? I looked all about it, but I couldn't see her. I knew I was in a dream. My legs were more or less planted, immovable in that moment.

It seemed real, though. I was just about to speak when I saw someone riding up on a great, thunderingly loud medieval charger. Instinctively, I started to hide, but my father didn't. Instead, he pulled himself up straighter and waited for the rider to come closer.

As my eyes stared upward, climbing the horse up to its rider, my mouth grew long and wide. The man wasn't human, something quite obvious at first sighting. For one thing, his skin was the color of my mother's cobalt blue coffee mugs, and for another, the man had three arms and three legs, one of which dangled down off the rear of the horse, draping over the animal's tail.

"What are you?" I screamed out, but neither my father nor the alien seemed to hear me. They were still staring at each other, each shocked, I guess, by the appearance of the other.

The rider yelled out something that sounded like, "Bisheewaworra."

Dad answered with something equally strange. I turned to look at him, but he was smiling up at the rider, and his hand was extended for a polite handshake.

"Dad, you can't be an attorney here," I said. "That *thing* is definitely not one of your clients."

Dad acted like he couldn't hear me. Neither did the blue guy, who was busy shaking my father's hand. The three-legged monster dismounted and bent over to check my dad's line. It was empty again, and the stranger thought that was hilarious. He threw his hand over Dad's shoulder, laughed, and began beating one of his limbs against my father's back.

Dad thought that was just fine, and he laughed, too. Then they both turned and walked away as if it weren't important they were leaving me behind without a backward glance or word.

I would have followed them, but my feet were still bound to the spot where I'd landed. I called out, entreating them to stop, but neither indicated that they'd heard me.

It is devastating to be ignored like that, especially when you haven't seen your parent in a week, and even more so when you're beginning to believe he might be dead. I wanted to throw my arms around my father. I wanted to hear him speak to me. But dreams don't let you guide them. They have their own rules.

I was anchored to that spot, as I said. All I could do was watch the rider's horse nibbling on some grass. The animal's reins were dangling on the ground. I thought the horse might step on them, but the animal seemed trained to avoid that. Whenever it seemed likely that a hoof would come down on a piece of leather, the horse simply shook its head and moved the rein away.

I sat down and began to talk to the animal. I think it could actually hear me, for its ears flipped back and forth at the sound of my voice. One of its eyes watched me, too. Since it had three of them, maybe the extra one was simply for sleeping, but it looked like it was staring at me.

The huge beast was very similar to an Earth horse. It had four legs ending in hooves, a neck with a heavy mane, a tail dangling down to the ground, and other horse-like appendages, except it was twice the size of any horse I'd ever seen, and its face was more triangular.

Its muzzle ended with yellowish teeth, just like a real horse, but those teeth were double-rowed, one set obviously meant for grazing grass, but the second, higher set looked sharp and predator-like. And, of course, three eyes, one of which, set above the other two and centered, looked like it was still watching me. Perhaps it was just as well the horse ignored me. That second set of teeth looked very dangerous.

As I sat watching the animal, a small bird flew down and sat on my shoulder. It was singing a song to me. I was enchanted. Not so the horse. It lifted up those dragging reins and charged right at me, its mouth making a beeline for my shoulder. I spun away from it, falling back onto the grass. The poor bird didn't move as quickly. The horse crunched its bones loudly.

At that moment, I wanted out of my dream desperately, but I still couldn't pull my feet away from the ground. I was trapped inside the strange environment with not a single defense. Oh, what I wouldn't have given at that moment for an epee or Sabre, my tools from my days of fencing.

Luckily, the horse, having finished its snack, resumed grazing, its third eye settling back into stare position. I wiped the sweat from my brow, took in a deep breath, and tried not to scream. What good would it do me, anyway, when apparently no one could hear me?

By the time the horse had shifted away from me, its top eye no longer staring my way, and I was starting to breathe in a normal fashion again, I heard a couple of female voices. One of them was my mother's.

"Mom!" I yelled.

The horse stamped one of its heavy hooves, which sent its head back toward me. Once more, the third eye stared at me. That time, I was positive the eye wasn't sleeping.

"Mom!" I called again, louder and more desperately.

The horse lifted up its head, shook it, and whinnied. Then, it trotted toward me, pounding those giant hooves closer and closer. I struggled, turning my feet right and left in an effort to free them, but it was as if they were stuck in cement. I reached down and tried to pry my toes from the soil, but still, they wouldn't budge. I was about to be run over by a horse the size of an army tank.

"Mom!" I cried out even louder and with more desperation.

Then I woke. My bed was wet from sweat. I wiped the sting out of my eyes, threw back the covers, and sat up. There was no horse, no castle, no moat, no mother. I wept as if I were four years old, wailing because I was not only safe from being squished but because, once more, I'd lost my parents, even if only in another dream.

When my tears had all come and gone, I slipped out of bed, showered, and sat down in the living room. I thought about the dream and about how real my parents had been. Where were they? What had happened to them? Why did I keep seeing them in that same strange place in dreams? I couldn't imagine my parents even visiting a castle, and my dad would be horrified at the idea of fishing. Such leisure activities were not for successful attorneys who ordered their fish plated and decorated with sophisticated sauces.

Outside, a screech owl announced its presence. In the distance, I heard a cat yowling for its mate. The faucet was dripping in the kitchen. I walked in, glanced about, and turned the handle sharply. The drip stopped. I heard a horse neighing. I turned to face the window, but I couldn't see anything. Outside, it was still dark — dark as the depths of a river. Had I really heard a horse? We didn't live in that kind of neighborhood. No horses were kept around here. It wasn't zoned for them. Was I still dreaming?

I walked to the front door, unhooked the night guard, unbolted the locks, and opened it. Everything outside looked normal. I could still hear the owl up in the old oak at the corner of our property. I stepped out to take a better look. I shouldn't have done that. My foot hit the water, and my body followed. Somehow, I'd fallen into a moat.

Chapter Five

I shut my mouth, not wanting to drown in what was obviously another dream. Good thing. The water smelled foul and was slimy on my fingertips as I paddled about, searching for a way to climb out. I guess moats aren't made with ladders. Steep sides covered with moss and a seaweed-smelling growth made the walls too slippery even to heave me out. I lay back and stared up at the stars.

"It doesn't matter," I told myself. "In a minute, I'll wake up. I'm probably still sitting in the living room, having fallen asleep in my dad's chair." So, I kept saying to myself over and over.

A huge shadow, dark and ominous, cracked my eyes open. I swear it was a dragon. Its round, green eyes peered down at me. Then, it let out a blast of fire that sizzled the water all around me.

I dived down into the depths. Dream or not, the pain of being boiled with fire was not something I wished to experience. I stayed down as long as I could, hoping the wind-flapping monster would disappear, but when I came up, it was still there.

It turned its head sideways, examining me as I gasped and choked on the putrid water. Then it dropped down from the sky, pierced both skin and clothes with its sharp claws, and soared me upwards.

"Let me go," I screamed. "Let me go!"

Do dragons speak English? I'd never heard that they could. All I could remember about them was that they dined on flesh — human flesh.

The monster had taken me up at least twenty feet, but like an idiot, I still flailed and kicked, seeking my freedom, even if that meant falling to my death.

"Benjamin, be still," I heard a voice yelling.

I froze and looked down. The voice was my mother's.

Apparently, the dragon took the call as a sign that it should descend. It did so much more quickly than I would have chosen had I not been clutched so firmly within its claws. I wasn't struggling, though. By then, I was overloaded. Too many dangers had been assaulting me, one after the other. I no longer had the sense to react to any of them in a sane manner.

The dragon alit, pushing me to the side as it did so. I stumbled and fell, but not from any great height. I was alive. Once I got my feet back onto the ground, I attempted to bolt away. Unfortunately, my effort didn't get me far. The dragon was still gripping me with its talons.

"Let him go, Garland," my mother ordered.

My captor let out a rude burst of flame, which, although it didn't scorch me, let me know that it could have burned me easily. I turned to face the monster, wanting to be prepared for the final blast, but it didn't come. Like one of those machines at the fair, the hooks of its long, skinny hands released me so abruptly that I stumbled again and landed in a heap on the ground.

"Garland," my mother scolded. "This is my son. You didn't have to be so rough!"

The dragon slipped its head underneath one wing. Either it was afraid of my mother or very embarrassed. For the first time, I sympathized with the creature. I knew the feeling well.

The dragon must have read my mind. Its eyes peeked out at me, and then it winked.

"Benjamin, are you all right?" my mother demanded with her usual tone that said I'd better answer distinctly and efficiently.

"I'm asleep. Otherwise, I think I'm okay," I told her, wondering at the vividness of my dreams. This time, I could even feel her hand touching my forehead. Her touch felt warm and familiar. And incredibly real.

"Poor darling," she cooed. "It is hard to believe at first. Your father and I . . ."

The dragon chose that moment to swing its heavy head around. It was clumsy as a … well, I guess, as a dragon. The weight of its head hit me like a speeding car. I whished off my feet, traveled about five feet in the air, and landed flat on my back — minus lung air.

While I was gasping for air, I opened my eyes. Unfortunately, the dragon was drooling. It peered down at me, its tongue dangling over my face. Perhaps I was only semi-lucid, but I had a sudden notion that the thing was about to kiss me.

I would have cried out. I would have slugged the monster. I would have liked to do a myriad of things, but all I could do was gasp and wave my arms about, trying to bring in air. Then, when, finally, I was able to inhale again, I pulled in a batch of air so sulfuric and stinky I expelled it almost as quickly as I took it in.

"AGGGG!" I cried out the moment I could speak. "Get this dragon off me!"

The thing had not only kissed me. It was slapping and then waggling its sticky green tongue across my face. Its breath was horrendous. It's saliva-spit even worse. And the whole idea of such a thing kissing me was so repulsive I wanted to puke.

"Garland, back away from him. Look what you've done!" my mother scolded as she walked toward me.

The dragon wasn't very obedient. Drool was still dribbling down into my face. I gagged and tried to inhale a puff of clean air. Then, seeing there was no way out of it but to sit up and move away from the thing, I put my elbows underneath me, pushed up, and got a second gooey, warm kiss.

"UGGG!" I yelled, pushing the huge head away. "Don't do that again. Never. Ever!"

The dragon took a step back. Its head tilted as it looked at me. "Blork?" it asked sadly.

How the heck was I supposed to know what *Blork* meant, you might ask. I was asking myself the same thing. But somehow, I knew. *Blork* was a dragon's way of saying, "I'm sorry. Will you forgive me?"

Dreams are funny that way. They send yellow flowers in the midst of a blizzard and bloom apple trees next to ripened fruit. Something entirely strange and impossible somehow becomes logical — or at least it seems logical in your brain as long as you remain asleep.

The fact that I suddenly knew Dragon Speech was, of course, one of those ridiculous idiosyncrasies. Yet, suddenly I not only knew for a fact that Dragons could speak, but I knew their language. In fact, based on the way my tongue had started formatting *Blork*-like words, I was pretty sure I spoke it, too. At least, that's what I rationalized as my mother held out her hand and pulled me up.

I wiped the slime off my face, took a breath of fresher air, and felt not one drop of fear at the fact that I was standing beside a creature twice as big as a Big Mack Truck.

Chapter Six

"Look at him standing there in his underwear. Why, he's barefoot, too. I told you we should have come over earlier. . ."

"Now, Martha. Leave the boy alone. I'm sure there's an explanation. Benjamin. Benjamin! Are you all right, lad?"

I blinked. I was no longer standing near a castle, a dragon, or a slimy–green moat. I was on the front porch of my parent's house in the dark, shivering.

My face was wet and sticky. My hair was dripping brownish swamp water down my naked chest. I was barefoot and . . .

"Mrs. Gillicutty. Mr. Gillicutty. What are you doing here?" I asked, considerably befuddled by the switch in scenery and characters. It was at that moment I realized that I was standing in front of the elderly couple in nothing more than a pair of boxer shorts.

I squatted down, then seeing that my new pose wasn't going to hide my lack of clothing, I quickly darted behind a bush, one with an abundance of snow-white camellias and shiny green leaves.

"We could ask that of you," Mr. Gillicutty said, turning off his flashlight so I'd come out of hiding.

When I didn't move, he gripped my arm and pushed me forward, back inside the house.

"What on earth were you doing outside at this hour of the night — especially dressed, or should I say, undressed like that?" he asked as we stepped inside.

His eyes were skimming me, not as if to see what a half-naked teenager's body looked like, but as if he could see into me and certify whether I was insane or not.

"Uh," I stuttered, blushing because Mrs. Gillicutty was there as well. "Please sit down. I'll be right back," I told them, and then I practically ran down the hall and into my room so I could slip into some pants and a shirt.

I suppose, if I'd been thinking straight, I would have stopped and combed my hair and brushed my teeth. But I'd fallen into an icy moat, dragon flown and drooled on, giant horse-attacked, and had strange visitations with my supposedly dead parents. I was in no condition to be sane at that moment. I took a deep breath, shook my head, and vowed to pretend as best I could.

When I returned to the living room, neither of them were there. I found them in the kitchen. Mrs. Gillicutty had made herself at home and was starting a pot of coffee. Her husband, as usual, was fussing at her that it was too late at night for such a thing and that I should be in bed. Both of them turned to look at me as I entered the room. Their eyes scanned me, checking that I was fully clothed and that I looked suitably normal again. I guess I passed.

"See, he's dressed now, isn't he?" Mrs. Gillicutty said, apparently just having scored the winning point of the argument. That settled, they both returned to what they'd been doing a moment before — Mrs. Gillicutty to the coffee and Mr. Gillicutty to placing some cookies on one of Mom's best dishes.

The Gillicuttys were our next-door neighbors, but they were more than just neighbors. The elderly couple had been my babysitters throughout my early years, my confidants whenever I felt like spewing, and my adopted grandparents. I realized now that I should have called them yesterday. I should have let them know I was home, but I'd been in shock. My head had been hurting, too. I just hadn't thought coherently.

"Sit down now, Benjamin," Mrs. Gillicutty ordered. "You look awful. Poor child. We should have been at your graduation. I told Harry that, but he wouldn't let me go. Ridiculous. He's such a mother hen, you know."

Mr. Gillicutty shook his head. "Now, Martha, don't get started again. You know what the doctor said. *No traveling.* Benjamin's school was several hour's drive away. The boy understands that, don't you, lad?"

I started to answer, but it was obvious they didn't need me in the conversation. Mrs. Gillicutty stamped her foot, clicked the coffee pot into the on position, and turned to glare at her husband.

"Doctors, what do they know? I'm fit as a fiddle," she argued. Then she walked over to me and patted me on the shoulder.

"What's wrong?" I asked, blinking again like a sleepy owl. "What does your doctor say?"

I stood up, wanting to do something, maybe hoping to solve Mrs. Gillicutty's problem somehow. Of course, I couldn't. I couldn't solve anyone's problems, not even my own.

"Sit down, Benjamin. Eat a cookie. You need some fattening up," Mrs. Gillicutty said, scolding me as if I were her own son.

I smiled at her and did as she said. Someone my age should have been offended and should have reared up and argued, but I was so adrift that it just felt good. I was grateful to hear someone telling me what to do.

"It's Martha's heart," Mr. Gillicutty said, taking the chair beside me and passing along the plate full of cookies. "Martha has a bad ticker. She knows it. She just won't admit it — or follow the doctor's directions like she should."

As I said, the Gillicutty had been raising me for many years. When they said eat, I usually did, whether I was hungry or not. I reached for a cookie and took a bite. These were getting stale. Carefully, I placed the other half on my saucer. If I tried to eat any more of it, I'd probably be sick.

My mom always kept cookies around, but she never nibbled on them. Neither did Dad. My parents treated cookies and candy as if they were merely essential decorations for a well-furnished kitchen. Unfortunately, that meant that although pretty, the stuff was usually pretty inedible and often older than a kindergartener.

Martha placed a mug in front of each of us. She turned to find no supply of milk in the refrigerator, but she knew where the powdered creamer was. She set a jar of it next to the bowl of sugar she'd already placed in the center of the table.

"Nonsense. My heart is just fine. That doctor doesn't know what he's talking about. He's hardly older than our Benjamin here. Just a kid."

The coffee had begun to drip into the pot, sending an amazingly delicious odor throughout the kitchen. My mouth salivated.

I started to get up to grab some napkins, but Mr. Gillicutty stopped me by placing his heavily veined and brown-spotted hand over mine. "Let her fuss over you, Benjamin. It makes her happy, lad. Let her fuss."

I sat back and nodded, watching as Mrs. Gillicutty brought over the napkins.

"Have some more cookies, Benjamin. That's a fresh box. They shouldn't be stale. You look like you need to eat some sweetness. Are you good? You're skinnier than a clothesline."

Ignoring her mention of the cookies, I thanked her as she set down three steaming mugs of coffee. I picked up mine and took a sip. It was scalding hot but every bit as good as it smelled.

I let out an "ah" of contentment, and the Gillicuttys both smiled.

"All right. Now you've had your waker-upper. Tell me what you were doing outside?" Mr. Gillicutty demanded. "It isn't safe, you know," he scolded me, just as if I were his Martha.

I smiled into my cup, keeping it level with my mouth so I wouldn't show my thoughts. Then I sighed as I tried to figure out what to say. "I don't really know," I admitted. "I guess I was sleepwalking. I haven't done that for years. I was in the middle of a dream. About my folks. They've been on my mind a lot, you know."

"Of course, they have, dear," Mrs. Gillicutty said, laying her hand on my shoulder as if that could chase away the shadows. "We're awfully sorry, Benjamin. We were devastated to hear."

She wiped a tear and pretended that she wasn't. Picking up her cup, she touched her lips to the rim and then set it down. "You got our flowers, didn't you? We sent them to the hospital. I wanted to go to see you, but the old man wouldn't let me do that either," she said, wiping a second tear with the napkin she'd crinkled up in her palm.

Mr. Gillicutty was shaking his head. I thought he was about to launch into how Martha couldn't travel again, but he didn't. He reached over for the sugar dish, slid it towards himself, and added three teaspoons of sugar to his cup.

Mrs. Gillicutty eyed his heaps of sugar. I thought she'd break into her usual tirade about it, but she didn't. She pursed her mouth, shook her head, and looked away. Then she paused to wipe her eyes again.

Meanwhile,, Mr. Gillicutty was stirring in the sugar — the coffee swirling around and around. I think he was pondering over what I'd just said because he didn't seem to be aware of what he was doing, and it was obvious that all the sugar had dissolved a good half-dozen rotations back.

I smiled, recalling what Dad used to say. He always called Mr. Gillicutty *the hummingbird,* claiming that our neighbor practically lived on sugar water.

"We should have visited you in the hospital, Benjamin. I'm sorry we didn't," Mrs. Gillicutty said out of the blue, repeating what she'd already said.

That brought her husband out of the depth of his thoughts. His face turned red, and his voice thundered. "You can't go nowhere, Martha. Benjamin understands that. We sent him the flowers. He knows our prayers were with him. Isn't that right, Benjie?"

I nodded and watched him take his first sip of coffee. He drank a couple of swallows, then set it down and stirred in another teaspoon of sugar. Mrs. Gillicutty used only milk in her coffee. Deprived of that, she was adding creamer. She grimaced when she took her first sip. I knew she hated the taste of the artificial stuff.

"Thank you for sending the flowers," I told them, not able to remember if I'd thanked them yet. "I really did appreciate it. They were pretty, too. I got your graduation present the week before. I can sure use the money. Thanks for everything."

They both smiled at me and took another sip of their coffee. I noticed that neither one of them took a cookie, even though they continued to urge me to eat.

"Don't you go spending that money on junk, now," Mr. Gillicutty said. "That's for college, young man. You use it wisely."

I nodded. "I'll spend it on books," I said. "Textbooks, I mean."

I knew things were tight for the elderly couple. Mrs. Gillicutty was constantly in and out of the hospital. The five hundred dollars the two had sent me must have cut deeply.

I stood up and hugged them, something I should have done a lot earlier. "I'm sorry," I said. "I should have written you. I should have called, too, but they wouldn't let me. No calls in or out. Weird hospital, huh? Anyway, I was going to come over tomorrow — I mean, this morning, later when it was light outside."

Mrs. Gillicutty set her mug down. Once more, she stretched out her hand and patted mine. "We understand, Benjamin. You've been sick, and then there's your folks. . . It's awful. Just awful. You can count on us, though. We're here for you. Anything you need, you ask. We don't have much money, but what we have is yours, dear. You know that."

Mr. Gillicutty nodded his head. He stretched out his right leg and reached down to massage the knee area. I knew he had trouble with his legs. They hurt him at night. Sometimes, he'd told me, he couldn't sleep at all because they twitched or just plain hurt so bad he'd have to get up and walk about. I started to comment, but what was there to say? I couldn't give advice about old knees. What did I know about the subject?

I picked up the other half of the dated cookie and shoved it into my mouth. It wasn't so bad dipped in coffee. The staleness wasn't as obvious.

Mr. Gillicutty left off massaging his knee for a moment to take another sip of his coffee. He used the movement to continue the conversation. "Now, Martha. The boy doesn't need money. He needs sleep. Why he's practically a ghost, he's so white. We better be gettin' home.

We didn't mean to bother you, Benjamin. It's the middle of the night, after all. We just heard an awful squeal in that tree. We thought the owl might have gotten one of the neighbor's cats or something. Then we saw you standing there in the doorway, looking like you'd seen… well like you were needin' us."

I nodded. Maybe that was what had woken me. That old owl. I smiled at them. "I did need you. I'm glad it was you who caught me sleepwalking. Better than the police or some stranger." I tried to chuckle over it, but it sounded flat.

"Thanks for waking me. If I'd frightened the newspaper girl or been seen by an early morning jogger, it would have been bad. I'm really glad you came over."

Mr. Gillicutty finished his syrup coffee, and carried his and Mrs. Gillicutty's mug to the sink. He rinsed them and set them inside the dishwasher.

"You go back to bed now. Sleep is good for you, but, Benjamin, maybe you'd better wear your clothes to bed for a while," he said, grinning.

I nodded and smiled back. Then I stood up, too, although I hadn't finished my coffee. "I just don't understand what's going on," I said. "Where are my parents?"

I knew they had no idea either, but their eyes were on me, and they were listening. I poured out my soul. "I keep having dreams about them, you know? Strange dreams, like they're somewhere else — in another world. That's silly, isn't it?"

"You mean like they're dead?" Mr. Gillicutty asked.

Martha, clinging to his arm as if she needed the support, started shushing him, but I shook my head.

"It's okay," I said. "I've faced that possibility. I don't understand what happened to them. I guess they must be dead. It's the only thing that makes sense. They wouldn't have stayed away this long. They wouldn't have left their clients . . ."

"Or you," Mrs. Gillicutty inserted, although I could tell from her eyes that she didn't actually believe that. The Gillicuttys were always discrete about my parents, but I knew the couple's feelings. They thought my parents took too little interest in my life. I suppose that's why the Gillicuttys had more or less adopted me. They probably figured I'd been neglected.

And it was true about my parents. They were good to me. I never lacked anything — except their attention.

I said goodnight to the Gillicuttys and walked the elderly couple out the front door. I know they stood on the doorstep waiting to hear the chain and bolt secured properly before they started walking back to their house. They were always like that. Good people. I was lucky to have them in my life and grateful that they cared.

I turned off the coffee pot, rinsed out the mug I'd used, and inserted it into the dishwasher. I tossed the cookies and turned off the kitchen light. Then I headed back to bed. As I slid under the sheets, I winced at the coldness. For some reason, the iciness of it reminded me of a tomb.

With that thought wedged in my brain, sleep didn't come easily. I listened to the sounds outside my window. A couple of mourning doves were cheering on the approach of daylight. A mockingbird chimed in, playing his wide variety of birdsong as if showing off to the doves. The paper girl tossed a heavy bundle in the driveway across the street. That was the last thing I remember before I opened my eyes and saw my father.

Chapter Seven

"Dad!" I screeched like a young boy. Ashamed, I repeated the word, speaking lower, in my normal range. "Dad, what's going on? Why do I keep dreaming about you and Mom? Where are you?"

Maybe a better question would have been where was I? With my eyes open and peering slightly past my dad, I could make out the background. I was pretty sure we were inside the castle I'd seen earlier. There were tapestries hanging on the walls and great swords and axes.

It was not a cheerful sight, especially since the nearest tapestry showed a giant ogre with an axe stuck in its head. The creature's eyes were wild with fear and rage, and it was dripping blood —no, spraying blood out of its head. Luckily, all the drops were merely threads in the tapestry, but it was certainly not a picture that one would normally find in a bedroom. Rather nightmare inducing.

"You're visiting us, Benjamin. Your mother has been working at her spells. She has summoned you, but she isn't strong enough yet to hold you long. That's why you keep boomeranging back too quickly."

It really seemed like my father was standing there. I blinked. Could a person blink in a dream? I pinched my arm. It hurt. Did that mean anything?

Dad wasn't touching me, as if afraid if he did, I'd slip away. I took a second look at him, and my mouth dropped open in disbelief. It wasn't only the background that looked unusual —my dad looked different. He had a beard, for one thing. He hadn't had one when I'd seen him in my other dream. And his clothes were weird. He was wearing brown tights and a long-sleeved lavender shirt with flounces. Frankly, he looked like he was dressed for Halloween, all the way down to his lavender, up-pointed-toed shoes.

"Dad, tell me what's going on? What is happening?"

He laughed exactly like he used to. At least, that hadn't changed. Dad's laugh was unique. It started at his mouth, which curled around the humor of things, then just kind of radiated outwards in ripples of it, like the way disturbed water furrows into ever-widening circles of movement.

With my father, the last thing that always occurred was the actual laugh itself. It was a procedure, but one I think he had no control over. Yet, like one of his carefully laid out court cases, you could trace the steps of its passing. The funny part is that even when you watched it blossom, even when you were prepared for its jolt, it carried you along with it. You couldn't help yourself. It didn't matter if you were angry about something; when Dad laughed, you just had to join in.

Yes, the sequence of the laughter was the same. And as he laughed this time, I fought it, like I usually did, but I was as helpless to its sweeping embrace as if I'd willed myself to comply. And once the laugh captured a person, you became lost in it. So I found myself splashing into the warmth of his laughter, even though a moment before, I'd felt like moaning and complaining about the oddness of everything.

I guess it was a good thing, though. It freed my father. He rushed closer, grabbed me up, and hugged me until I could scarcely breathe. He was much stronger than he used to be. I discovered that because he was crushing me with his enthusiasm. Gasping for breath, I tried to pull away.

"Adam, you're squishing him," came my savior's voice.

I breathed in deeply and turned around, eager to hug my mother.

"It worked. I brought him back again," she said to either my father or me. I took in the expression on both their faces. It was the usual thing when they were together. Embarrassingly, my parents were madly in love with each other. I looked away immediately.

Most of my friends had parents who wouldn't even talk to each other. Half of them had divorced or separated parents. Nobody I knew had parents who exchanged lovelorn looks that mortified their kids to death. It just wasn't done.

Yet, I didn't interrupt. I'd discovered over the years I frankly couldn't. Impatiently, I waited until they got over it and noticed me again.

I think I half expected my father to turn and say, "You still here?" but he didn't. Instead, he glanced over at me and said, "Listen, Benjamin. You're going to have to make a choice. Your mother can't hold the portal open very long, and we don't know how lengthy your stay will be. Maybe a minute, an hour, a day. Eventually, you're going to have to choose — one life or the other."

My mother was clutching my father's arm, holding him back somehow. From what? And what on earth was Dad talking about? Portal? Choose? What life?

My mother, still gripping his arm as if this was a life and death case she was arguing, and she was pleading for her client. "You're confusing him Adam. Look at his face. He doesn't even believe he's here."

Dad sighed in the way he always did when I wasn't able to keep up with the speed of his thinking. Usually, that meant he was about to walk away from me, leaving me to feel stupid. In preparation, I fidgeted, shifting to lean against the wall — the one without the bleeding ogre.

"What's there not to understand?" he argued. "He's obviously not in the old world. We're somewhere else, in a much friendlier world, one with no war or pollution. No taxes, too," Dad said, grinning like those silly happy face stickers long ago teachers always plastered on good papers.

My mother turned his face toward her. She planted a kiss on his chin. That, of course, made Dad drop his eyes to her. His lips followed.

Yick! Right in front of their son. I checked out the ogre again and waited.

"But, Adam, dear love. It took you a while to make that decision. Remember?" my mother reminded him, slipping her arm through his so he could beam at her some more, which led, of course, to another kiss on the lips.

Meanwhile, I'm not certain this happened, but I think the ogre winked at me. How could he, with an axe deeply implanted in his head and blood dripping from his wound in dark, red stitches of yarn? Good question, but from my angle, the way things had been so crazy, anything was possible.

I looked back at my parents to see if they were finished with their romance stuff. They weren't kissing anymore, but I could see their eyes still staring into each other's souls.

Uncertain if I wanted to continue studying the violent death of a winking ogre, I took a moment to examine my mother's appearance. I had to admit she looked wonderful. The pale green of her full-length velvet dress did something to her eyes. She appeared younger than I'd ever seen her, more beautiful even than before. She really did not look like a county district attorney. To be honest, my mother looked like an actress — a famous movie star in the role of Genevieve, wife of King Arthur.

I swallowed hard. I know that sounds awful for a kid to say about his mother, but although she wasn't in the same class as Sharon Doister, I'd only be honest in admitting that Mom was very attractive — for her age, I mean. Maybe, long ago, she was a Sharon Doister, stealing all the young guys' eyes. She certainly had my father wrapped around her finger.

Reading what I'd just written, I groan with embarrassment. I see it didn't come out right at all. I sound like I was accusing my mother of being a femme fatale or something. She was never like that. She was too into her court cases, wearing those silly little glasses at the end of her nose, getting smudges on her face from the black of the copy machine, crinkling up her forehead from concentrating too. hard . . .

All I meant to say was that my mother looked good.

I was busy concentrating on getting that right in my mind when I realized that my parents had returned their attention to me. I think my father had even said something.

"What?" I asked, wiping a bit of spiderweb off my elbow. I took a peek around, wondering what spiders looked like in this world. Then, just to be cautious, I stepped away from the wall.

"He's not listening again, Sarah. I told you that's his problem," my dad said with his usual irritation at my wandering mind.

I shifted and leaned back against the wall. I could deal with spiders. I couldn't deal with my father's constant disappointment. That was much harder to fight.

Chapter Eight

The sun was streaming through the window when I woke. At first, I was a bit confused about where I was. I sat up in bed and looked about. No ogre with an axe in the head, being the star of a hanging tapestry, only a baseball banner cheering on the local team. My eyes toured the room, reacquainting themselves with the plastic dinosaur model on the top of the bookcase, the globe of the heavens I'd gotten for my fifth birthday, and my telescope, still perched in position as if ready for Saturn's rings to come back in sight.

I rubbed my eyes, yawned, and crawled out of bed. My old house slippers were on the floor beneath me. I pushed my toes in and wiggled. The slippers were too tight. I figured that was probably true of most of my closet full of clothes. I'd rarely lived at home — rarely dropped in for a visit over the past five or six years.

I made my way into the shower, shaved the few sparse hairs that grew on my chin, and said "hello" to a brand new toothbrush, knowing that Mom must have purchased supplies for me.

I breakfasted on a couple of boiled eggs and some canned corn. Then, as I ate, I started a wish list of groceries I'd need if I were going to stay long.

Then it hit me. Where else could I go?

Dad had planned to give me a job at his law firm over the summer. I had nothing else lined up, and school didn't start for another three months. I wondered if I still had a job at the firm. The thought kicked me in the head. Shouldn't I be wondering where my parents were instead of thinking about me again?

I visited their bedroom, not touching anything, just reacquainting myself and, I suppose, making sure my parents weren't hiding in it. Of course, their room was empty. A layer of dust covered everything, including the bathroom counter where their toothbrushes hung, left behind when they'd journeyed off to celebrate my graduation from high school.

As I toured their personal space, feeling like an invader of their private domain, I wondered idly why the cleaning crew hadn't come to dust. Normally, like clockwork, they came each Wednesday, but it was obvious they hadn't been there the day before. Did cleaning companies scan the paper and take a vacation when their customers disappeared?

I pulled open each of the drawers, one at a time, checking to see if there were any clothes missing. It looked like all my parents' possessions were still neatly folded. Dad's boxers had been rolled into individual bundles., each one carefully inserted in its own separate cell. Mom's drawer of intimates looked the same. Neither had more than a couple of empty spaces. I'd probably find that underwear in the dirty clothes hamper.

I checked the walk-in closets, riffling through the three-piece suits and the ladies' dresses and jackets. How would I know if things were missing? I couldn't recall every outfit, of course, but I found no empty hangers, and my parents' matching suitcases were still tucked away in the specially designed cupboards at the rear of the closet.

My mother's dresses smelled of her perfume. I breathed in the scent and wiped a tear. Mom was always too busy to chat, as she constantly promised we would, but that didn't matter now. Just having her in the house, having her wear those horn-rimmed glasses bent over a law book, seemed a pleasure that had been unfairly stolen from me.

My father's suits carried his scent, as well. Cedar. Dad believed that moths were lying in wait for a careless moment without protection. Mom's side of the closet was lined, too, but her dresses didn't smell of it. Dad's reeked of cedar.

My father and I were often at crosscurrents, but still, I missed him. There had always been that faint chance that I might one day do something right. There was a possibility that one day, I'd achieve his approval. Would I see a smile of pride flash across his face, a smile like I'd seen on the other parents' faces at graduation?

The realization that I couldn't earn it now and would never see his approval, just about did me in. I retreated from the closet, slammed the door, and rushed into the bathroom, where I had a long-overdue nose blowing.

Later, with my face washed and my eyes only slightly red, I journeyed into their office. They shared that room as they shared the bedroom — not, of course, because they had to. There were extra, unused rooms in the house. They kept them for guests, although we rarely had any. My grandparents were dead, and we had a deficit of aunts and uncles. Evidently, I came from a long line of single children.

One wall of the office was set up as a library. From ceiling to floor, shiny leather texts filled the shelves. It was a law library, kept up with great diligence. Dad used to boast that he had everything at home just in case he needed it. Both he and Mom spent most of their spare time reading those volumes. I'd peeked inside one and found the writing to be so small I almost had to squint. And it was boring stuff — like reading a dry, old history book — perhaps even more so, for there were no pictures or captions of any kind.

Mom and Dad kept two desks in the room on opposite sides. That always surprised me, although I suppose they preferred that particular positioning for better concentration. They had separate phone lines and individual computers, file cabinets, and even two fax machines, although I wasn't sure they ever used them anymore. My parents might as well have had separate offices, except I imagined when I wasn't around, they probably took frequent breaks with lots of kissing and hugging.

I headed first for Mom's desk. I had no idea what I was looking for, but I felt that I had to go through the motions. I found an envelope with several hundred-dollar bills. I took one, remembering that I'd need to buy some food that day. I found the same thing on Dad's desk. I returned Dad's envelope and the money inside and continued my search.

The file cabinets were locked, but I knew where the keys were kept. I glanced inside the big metal drawers, but there was nothing that called to me, just names of people I'd never heard of. I closed and locked up the cabinets and went to the safe. It was behind my picture, the one painted of me from a snapshot taken when I'd won first place at a horse show years ago. I set the picture down on the ground and dialed in the formula. It was set to my mother's birthday, so it was always easy to remember.

Inside, I found copies of my parents' wills. I pushed them back inside, not wanting to read them yet. There were several other envelopes with money inside. I didn't bother to count the bills. I knew my parents were wealthy. Money had never been a problem. I shoved the envelopes back inside and shuffled through the rest. There wasn't much. Deeds to some property — several I hadn't known about, stock certificates in various companies, some bonds, and my mother's good jewelry. There was no letter to me — no explanation of where they might have gone.

I sighed, returned the papers, closed and locked the safe, and rehung my picture.

Where had my parents gone? Why had they disappeared? It was frustrating not to know, not to understand what had happened to them.

My search had only uncovered one single clue — a key that belonged to a safe deposit box. Could that box possibly hold the answers? I fingered the key nervously, wondering how I was supposed to find out which bank it went to. There was a number on the key — no other information. I went back to the file cabinets, looking for files on banks. In the bottom drawer of Mom's desk, I found some statements. I suppose I should have glanced at the totals, but I didn't. I just copied down the name of the bank and placed the documents back where I'd found them.

Then, it was lunchtime. I found a can of tuna, and even though there wasn't any bread, I was searching for the can opener (Dad hated the electric kind) when the phone rang. The Gillicuttys were inviting me over for lunch. Delighted by the offer, I gave a cheer and put the tuna back on the shelf. Then I went out to the rose garden to pick some flowers for Mrs. Gillicutty.

We had meatloaf, fresh green peas from their garden, green beans from their neighbor, and biscuits that melted in your mouth with or without the honey butter Mr. Gillicutty insisted I try. For dessert, there was a homemade peach pie made from peaches they'd harvested from their own tree back in August and then frozen in a sugar glaze. Mrs. Gillicutty made incredibly delicious pies, and her peach pie was my favorite.

After lunch, I told the Gillicuttys about searching the house and about the key I'd found. I explained how I'd discovered which bank my parents used, too. Mr. Gillicutty, almost immediately, offered to drive me downtown so I could check to see if the key would open their safe deposit box. I was happy to take him up on the offer. I'd been wondering how I was going to get to the bank.

You see, I still didn't have a driver's license. That was a considerable embarrassment for someone my age. I was probably the only high school graduate who had never been behind the wheel of a car, but my parents had been firm about the subject. They didn't believe kids should drive. Now, what was I going to do about the situation — parentless and therefore unable to get the permission needed for a learner's permit? I had a good car in the garage, but no idea how to use it, and our house was a long way away from any public transportation.

I didn't bother the Gillicutty with my problems. It was enough that they'd agreed to help me check the safe deposit box. Maybe, if I worked my cards right, we might stop on the way back and pick up some food. That would help a lot.

Mr. Gillicutty and I cleared up the dishes. Then, as they were loaded into the dishwasher and Mrs. Gillicutty was sitting comfortably in her recliner with the TV going, we headed out. Mr. Gillicutty drove up to the First Interstate and dropped me off because he had an errand to run. Feeling far less brave than when I'd pictured myself entering the bank with Mr. Gillicutty at my side, I pushed back my shoulders and headed inside.

I guess all banks are more or less the same — heavy carpeting on the floor, quiet like it's a library or a mortuary, and sternly serious looks on everyone's faces. Does money make people solemn? First, Interstate could have been the poster boy for it. I walked over to the information booth. A guy, only a couple of years older than I was, escorted me to the counter where the safe deposit check-in was. I told the bank teller my name and the situation and showed her my key.

I thought that would be the end of it, but several people came over, including the bank manager. They all wanted to inspect the key like it was an antique or something. Each person, including the president, turned the key around and around, held it up to the light, and then passed it on for someone else to examine.

Finally, the manager said, "I'm sorry, son. This key isn't one of ours. I don't think it belongs to *Country Freedom Bank,* either. You might try the transportation center. It's possible that it's a locker key."

Feeling like a fool, I pocketed the key and started to walk away. The manager called me back.

"Benjamin," he said, writhing his hands as if I made him nervous. "Your parents do have an account here. Under the circumstances, I'd be glad to let you take some money out if you need it." The man had begun to sweat as if the bank were hot, but I could feel the air conditioner running. I looked into his eyes and saw his worry that I'd take him up on the offer. I guess it wasn't easy to let go of money, or was it something else — something like the suspicious nature of my parents' disappearance?

I thanked the man and headed for the exit, feeling the eyes of everyone following me as I made my way out the back door and into the parking lot. Mr. Gillicutty wasn't back yet. I sat down on a bench and waited. The bench was under an elm tree. Its leaves kept rustling with the light breeze of the day. It reminded me of my dream, the one where my mother had been outside with a dragon named Garland.

When Mr. Gillicutty's car drove up, I jumped in. "Do you think we could stop on the way home at a grocery store so I could pick up a few things?" I requested.

He smiled. "I was hoping you'd ask. There are a few things I want to buy, too. Martha doesn't like it when I shop without her, but I figure that since you need stuff, she can't possibly complain about it."

We both laughed. I knew Mr. Gillicutty adored his wife, but he worried about her a great deal. She wasn't supposed to do half the things she did. The doctor wanted her to rest more, but that was something Mrs. Gillicutty didn't like to do.

Earlier, I'd thought that a hundred dollars would buy a whole grocery cart full of food. Boy, was I wrong? By the time I'd picked up all the things I was sure I needed, the bill came to $145. I plopped the hundred down and used my emergency money, then collected the change. It was obvious I might need to take the bank manager up on his offer sooner than I'd envisioned.

We loaded the things in the trunk and headed off after making a brief stop for an ice cream cone at the corner shop. I told Mr. Gillicutty it was my treat.

I paid, but then he bought us each a chocolate candy bar, giving me a wink and saying, "That's for later, Benjie."

We stopped in to check on Mrs. Gillicutty. She was sound asleep, still in her chair. I offered to carry the groceries over to my house, but Mr. Gillicutty wouldn't hear of it.

"I'll drive you, Benjie. You've got an awful big load."

An hour later, I had everything put away. I stuck in the leftovers from lunch that the Gillicuttys had sent with me, poured myself a cola, and sat down at the table. The crickets were out in full that evening. They were already singing their summer songs. I listened for a while. Then I got up and turned on the radio. The silence of the big house had begun to eat away at me.

That night, there was nothing on TV. I put in an old video and watched a movie I'd seen several times. It was too familiar. It didn't hold me. My thoughts kept drifting off, wondering about my parents, wondering if this was going to be my life from then on. Alone and lonely.

The screech owl was back. He silenced the crickets. The night didn't sound as friendly as it had earlier. I slipped a sweatshirt over my head and began to pace, fingering the mysterious key. Could it really be from the transportation center? Would it fit one of the lockers? But why? My dad would never go to a place like that. My mother, too. They put locker stuff in the trunk of their BMWs, one of which still occupied the garage.

My stomach was feeling queasy. Maybe meatloaf twice in a row wasn't a good idea. I went looking for some over-the-counter tablets in my parent's bathroom. Inside the cabinet, where I hadn't thought to look, I found an envelope. I ripped it off, tore it open, and started to read.

Chapter Nine

Dear Agnes,

Our son is coming home on Friday. Please make sure that the sheets in his bedroom are freshly clean, and that you dust extra well in there. I have placed a variety of toiletries in his medicine cabinet. Check it and see if there's anything else you can think of that he might need. You remember Benjamin; he's seventeen now. I'm sure there are things I may have forgotten. Thank you.

As always,

Sarah Thorne

My hands were shaking as I finished reading. Disappointment was thick. I'd thought this was the note for me, the reason, the destination . . .

I dropped the letter into the sink and clutched at the basin with both hands. "Where are you, Mom?" I whispered. "Why have you left?"

I completely forgot my need for medicine. I walked back into my parents' room and sat down on their bed. That was something I'd never have done if Mom were home. No one was allowed to sit on the antique quilt. Pink and yellow patches set inside a stark white outer frame – the quilt was supposed to be over a hundred years old.

With my finger, I traced one faded diamond shape. The material was kind of wrinkled as if its maker had twisted it purposefully. It was my mother's treasure, bought long before I was born. I felt guilty sitting on it, yet I resisted the urge to get up. If Mom had cared so much about preserving the stupid thing, she shouldn't have left me here all alone with it.

I was rarely invited into my parent's room. I'd never had the chance to really examine the quilt, to try to see what my mother saw in its delicate stitchery. I guess it was beautiful. Someone had spent hours putting the pieces together. A task of love, my mother probably would have said. And then they'd given it to a family member to be cherished, I supposed. How had my mother gotten it? Why had someone given it up? Did it matter now? Its owners were probably long gone, dead, and this quilt was all that remained.

And my mother — was she dead as well, leaving only an antique quilt as her memento?

Once again, my parents' room proved too much for the ache inside me. Tears flooded my eyes. I swallowed them back, but they wouldn't be stopped. So, at last, I simply let them flow. What did it matter? I was alone. Who would see my tears? Who would care?

"Benjamin."

It was my mother's voice. I looked up, but she wasn't there. Was I going mad?

"Benjamin. We love you. Really, we do."

That was all I could take. I stood up and ran out of their bedroom and into mine. I slammed the door behind me. Then I threw myself down on the bed and gave into my misery.

That night, I had no dreams. I woke up in the morning feeling refreshed and ready to solve any and all mysteries. The only problem was that I still couldn't drive. I ate breakfast, waited until ten, and then called the neighbors.

"How would you like lunch out on the town?" I asked Mrs. Gillicutty.

She giggled like a young girl. "Are you asking me for a date, young fellow?"

"Sure, do you have to ask permission . . . or should we include your husband?"

She giggled again. "Harry, it's Benjamin. He wants to know if we'd like to have lunch in town. Is that okay?"

Mr. Gillicutty came onto the phone and said, "You got enough money, Benjie? Maybe you should be a little careful with it. You don't know how long . . ."

I could hear his wife telling him to stop. He covered the phone for a minute. When he came back on, he said, "All right, Benjie. Martha is all excited about this date you two are planning. What time should I pick you up?"

"Eleven thirty?"

"Sure, but why don't we make it eleven, and you can stop off at the transportation center and check if that key fits?"

Mr. Gillicutty was a prince. I told him so before I hung up. Then, I scrambled to find something nice enough to dine in. None of the clothes hanging in my closet fit. I had only what I'd had on for graduation and a couple of old T-shirts that were probably too small. I'd worn my good clothes the day before. I really didn't want to wear them again. Then I thought of my dad's walk-in closet full of suits.

I dreaded going back in there. I didn't want to hear any more voices, but I needed something to wear. Urgency drove me forward.

My parents' room had a lovely picture window that opened out into the backyard. I went to stand in front of it so I could admire the

68

dark green of the lawn and the shade trees full of fat new leaves. A robin was poking its head in the grass, looking for worms, no doubt. It was a male with a full breast of red. I admired it for a moment before turning away.

"The time has come, the walrus said," I murmured my favorite *Alice in Wonderland* poem to still the rapid beating of my heart. I opened the closet door and stepped inside. The smells of my parents inundated me with memories, but no voices played with my mind. I turned to face my father's side and parted the rows of suits.

I'd always thought of Dad as being super tall. I'd never thought I could fill his pants, but I did. He was slender, too. That helped. An extra buckle tighter on the belt, and I was looking sharp. The jacket was a little lengthy in the arms, but when I threw my shoulders back and stood the way I should, the fit wasn't bad. The socks worked, too, but the shoes — no way. Dad had narrow feet. I'd inherited my mother's wider foot. I couldn't walk two steps without wincing. I tried pair after pair. Then I put my old tennis shoes back on and shrugged. I'd done the best I could.

Precisely at eleven, the car drove up, and I got into the back. Mrs. Gillicutty oohed and aahed about how handsome I looked. Mr. Gillicutty just grunted and said, "His shoes didn't fit?"

When I shook my head, he nodded. "It's hard to fill a father's shoes. We'll stop off at Kenner's. They'll have something in your size."

I'd earlier grabbed a couple hundred from my mother's drawer, but I gulped a bit at that. New shoes? Weren't they pretty expensive? Yet, there really wasn't any alternative. If I was going to see if the job at the legal office was still open for me, I'd need to look good. I had the suit business figured out, but shoes… I'd have to splurge on them. I definitely couldn't get by with a pair of old tennis shoes.

I closed my eyes and wondered again where the shoes I'd worn for graduation had ended up. Had they been lost in transit or misplaced at the hospital? Perhaps Susan Doister had taken them as a memento. As ridiculous as the thought was, it brought a smile.

We stopped off for the shoes first. I picked out a pair of black and, upon Mr. Gillicutty's insistence, a pair of brown. Then, wearing one pair and carrying the other, we walked over to the transportation center and searched the lockers.

Mrs. Gillicutty sat down at the window where she could watch the buses and trains coming in. She started up a conversation with a young mother and child before we'd even walked away.

"Figures. That woman just loves to talk," Mr. Gillicutty grumbled, but I could tell he was so proud of her that he was halfway bursting with it.

The bank manager was right. My mystery key did look like a locker key. We matched the number on it to one of the smaller cubbies down at the bottom. Then I placed the key into the keyhole, twisted it, and the small door flew open. Inside was an envelope. I reached for it and pulled it out.

To my darling on her birthday, it said.

"What? Oh, no! It's not a letter to me," I told Mr. Gillicutty. "It's from my father to my mom. Her birthday is next Monday. I'd forgotten."

"Well, why did your father put it here? Open it up. Let's see what it says."

It felt wrong to open something not addressed to me, but I'd gone this far. I ripped apart the envelope and looked inside. There was a small note and another key.

Darling, this year, I'm not making it easy for you.

There's something lovely at the end of this, but

you're going to have to hunt for it — unlike last year

when you found your present in my jacket.

To use this key, go to the safe under our bed.

"A safe under the bed? I didn't know about that," I said, considering. " I do remember last year. Dad was really bugged with Mom because she found her birthday necklace two days early. He must have built a scavenger hunt for Mom to keep her from discovering her present. Interesting, but I'm afraid it doesn't have a thing to do with their disappearance."

Mr. Gillicutty sat on the bench across from the locker. His eyes darkened. "It doesn't matter, Benjamin. When the time comes, you'll know."

For a moment, he sat quietly, reflecting. He tilted his head and stared. The station's big picture window gave a beautiful view. The pale blue of the sky was filled with puffy, cotton ball clouds, the kind that often filled up with rain and then turned dark and ominous.

"Maybe this is just a warm-up for your discovery, Benjamin," Mr. Gillicutty said. "You're sure getting to know your parents better."

He patted me on the shoulder, leaving his hand there for a moment, long enough for me to feel the warmth of it.

"How about we go tell Martha what we found?" he added. "I bet she's curious, if she's not involved already in whatever story that young mother has to tell her."

I smiled, but I wasn't really into learning about someone else's misfortune. I forced my smile full so that Mr. Gillicutty would see I could handle things on my own, but I felt all shaky inside. My stomach was knotting up again. The headaches were coming back.

I sighed, stood up, and then paused to rub the side of my head, trying to massage away the pain. That helped a little, but the truth is that I'd thought I was about to solve a mystery. Instead, I'd landed right back at square zero.

Chapter Ten

Mr. Gillicutty was right. His wife was very much in the midst of a long, drawn-out story about how mean a young woman's husband had been to her and how life was going to improve as soon as Carol went home to her folks.

The woman was still young, maybe only a couple of years older than me. She was pretty, too, in a coarse kind of way. Her hair needed touch-ups where she'd streaked it. The blonde roots with the midnight black of the rest of her head made her look diseased. Her face was chalky as if she'd been sick or stayed inside too much. But she had a kind smile. I hoped Mrs. Gillicutty's advice would help her.

However, Mr. Gillicutty cut that off with a few choice words. "You ready to never see your young gent again?" he demanded.

The woman, glancing over at Mrs. Gillicutty, emphatically spouted, "Yes," but then hesitated. She jostled the baby in her lap and stared down at the child for a minute. Her eyes turned doubtful. With one finger, she scratched at her blondish roots. "Well, I don't know. He's not always mean. Sometimes he's…"

Mr. Gillicutty eyed her sternly. "Did he ever hit you?"

She shook her head. "He would never do that. But he's always saying mean things."

"I see. Let me ask you this. If you go home to your parents, can he afford to come get you and the baby?"

The woman bit her lip. She crossed and uncrossed her legs. One jean leg had a rip across the knee. I didn't know if that was the latest fashion or a sign of poverty.

"Well, no," she said, twisting her purse strap nervously. "But that's his fault," she said, looking at Mrs. Gillicutty as if she were the one who had made this decision. "If he earned more . . ."

Mr. Gillicutty sat down across from the woman. He nodded his head as if he understood completely, but his eyes looked unconvinced.

"It's one of the hardest things to do to hold a relationship together. Me and Martha — we're the lucky ones. We've had forty-seven years. Been several spats, of course. I'm sure she wanted to go home to her parents, but they died early in life, leaving her an orphan. Maybe that helped us stay together. Maybe if she'd run home to her parents each time we argued, we wouldn't have made it. I don't know."

Mrs. Gillicutty was smiling at her husband. She'd already forgotten her battle to win the woman's independence. The young woman kept looking back and forth between the Gillicuttys. I think she was seeing how much they loved each other. She looked down at her baby, gave the little one a kiss, and then sighed loudly.

"Maybe I should call him and give him a chance?" she asked, looking at Mr. Gillicutty instead of at the woman she'd been talking with all this time.

"That's a good idea, Carol. Give him another chance," Mrs. Gillicutty urged. "Here, I'll hold the baby while you talk with him."

It was just like them to get involved with a complete stranger. Some people just had that much goodness in their souls that it seemed to fall off in waves that soothed the world. Get a thousand Gillicuttys and sprinkle them about and the whole universe would change. It would soon glow with love.

While I was thinking all that, Carol, who had moved a couple of rows away but was sitting where she could keep an eye on the three of us and her baby, sat talking to someone on her cell phone. You could see the tears streaming down her face, but she was smiling, and when she got off the phone, she came skipping over to us. "He still loves me. He wants me to come home. Thank you. Thank you so much."

She took her baby back, grabbed up her suitcase, and went running off, glowing with happiness,

"Well done," said Mrs. Gillicutty, smiling up at her husband. "Well done, my love."

As we left the transportation center, I studied the way the Gillicuttys walked together. They almost leaned on each other, like they were part of a whole. I guess that's what my parents would be like one day — the way they already acted. It was a good thing. I hoped one day I'd find something similar.

At the restaurant I'd chosen, we had a lovely Italian meal with green salads and their special combos, which included raviolis, lasagna, and spaghetti. While we were munching on the house's breadsticks, Mr. Gillicutty and I explained about the key and what it had revealed.

"How sweet!" Mrs. Gillicutty exclaimed. "Are you going to find out what he bought her?"

"You mean, follow the trail?" I asked.

I thought about the safe under the bed, the one I hadn't known about. Of course, I'd open that, even though I was sure there wouldn't be a letter in it — at least not one for me. But I didn't know how much further I'd go with this thing. It was obviously just a matter between my mother and father. I wasn't supposed to be involved.

I put down my fork and wiped my face with the cloth napkin. "It means I've run out of clues as to where my parents are," I said. "Where do you think they could be? Do you think they're . . . they're dead?"

Mrs. Gillicutty put down her fork. She blotted her mouth, even though she wasn't a messy eater, and never dropped sauce anywhere, not even when eating spaghetti. "Oh, Benjamin," she said. "Don't give up. There's always hope. I do know one thing, though; if they can come back to you, they will."

I fingered my fork, wanting to pick it up and eat more ravioli, but I knew I couldn't right then because Mrs. Gillicutty's words were choking me. Could that be true? I thought about all the dreams I'd been having and how my dad had said they were staying there in that castle, wherever it was. They'd told me I'd have to choose.

Mrs. Gillicutty had said my parents would come back if they could, but I doubted that. Not if they had each other. Not if they'd found something they wanted more.

Truth is often bitter. Sometimes, it's almost impossible to swallow, but it's always better than lying to yourself. The truth is that I didn't think my parents were ever coming back. I wasn't sure what had happened to them, but whether they'd chosen their fate or not, the odds were they wouldn't be returning.

I told the Gillicuttys that, and a great sadness stole into their eyes. Neither of them disputed what I'd said. They remained silent, and then Mr. Gillicutty placed his hand over mine. "We will be your family, Benjamin, for as long as you need us or want us. We will be your family. Okay?"

The back of my eyes was burning. I swatted at the tears before they could fall, but Mrs. Gillicutty, grabbing up my other hand, ended all my defenses. I wept then, right inside Gino's Italian Restaurant. I hoped no one saw me. In a minute, I pulled myself back together, thanked the Gillicuttys, and used the cloth napkin to erase all evidence.

Then, as if there'd been a signal given, we each reached for our fork and began eating again. After that, after a pause of spaghetti slurping, the Gillicuttys told me to call them Martha and Harry. It made me feel older, like I'd reached a point of passage. I suppose that life doesn't run smoothly, but it does always flow forward.

As I paid for our meal, I held Martha's hand. Harry kept his on my shoulder. "This is our honorary grandson who's paying today," Harry told the cashier as I forked over fifty bucks. "He treated us to a fine meal at your restaurant, and we're grateful that he wants to do that."

Martha added, "Benjamin just graduated from high school, and we're really proud of that, too."

The cashier didn't know what to say. He just nodded and handed back my change.

"Need anything?" Harry asked.

I shook my head and slid into the backseat of their car. Then the Gillicutty's, my new family, drove me home.

Of course, the first thing I did, even before I changed out of Dad's suit, was to check out the safe underneath the bed. There was a pillowcase over it. That's apparently why I hadn't noticed it before, although I hadn't thought to look under the bed. I pulled the safe out, plopped it down on the bed, and inserted the key. Perfect fit.

Inside, there was nothing but an envelope. I held it up to the light. It held another key. This one wasn't like the locker key. It was thicker and sturdier. I turned it over in my hand, wondering if it was a safe deposit box key.

I sighed. I didn't want to go back to the bank. The thought of going through what I'd already done felt like throwing myself at a brick wall just for the fun of it. All those employees eyeing me, the bank president giving me that look of pity. Yet, if the key really were the one that opened my parents' safe deposit box, might there still be a letter inside, one written for me? I had to try. I had to continue the search.

I called Harry and filled him in on what I'd found. He offered to take me the next day. I thanked him and was just hanging up the phone when the doorbell rang. It couldn't be the Gillicuttys. I rushed to the door and without pausing to check on identity, flung it open.

It was only a deliveryman with a package for me. I signed and tugged the heavy box inside. It was my stuff from Pinecrest Academy. At least I had my own clothes then. I locked the door, dragged the box down the long hall into my room, and began to unpack.

Chapter Eleven

That night, the dream came again. I opened my eyes and saw my parents dancing at a party. There was music, the classical kind, and everyone was in a costume with masks and shiny satins or velvet gowns. The men all wore pointed shoes like my father's and tights that showed off their calves. Strangely, although the men wore long cloaks that covered their bodies with swirls of fabric as they danced, their arms remained uncovered. Perhaps that was because all of them displayed muscles tight and hard as tree trunks.

The women let their hair drape over their shoulders, long and flowing, yet contained by headbands that flaunted a sparkling jewel on their forehead. Their gowns, unlike the males', showed no sight of skin. Their legs and arms were covered, wreathed loosely with the heaviness of cloth. None of them wore either makeup or glasses. All of the women were attractive, even the older ones, but especially several youthful ones who giggled behind fan-covered mouths when they saw me staring.

I looked away and studied the dance. Musicians were playing instruments that looked like lutes, strumming them softly to a slow, haunting rhythm. The dancers were revolving between each other, passing partners with smiles. Their faces held a look of elegant gentility, almost an echo of the music being played.

I felt out of place. This was obviously someone else's dream world. I didn't belong.

I was moving away, heading for the gardens, which I could see through a side passageway when my mother intercepted me. "You are back again, my son. Welcome."

"What's going on, Mom?" I asked, turning to look at her. "Why do I keep having these dreams?"

Her lips parted. They were pale. She wore no lipstick for the first time I could remember. Even when I'd lived at home, she'd never come to breakfast without lining her lips in it. The thought unsettled me as if she were standing in front of me nude or something. I closed my eyes and mentally kicked myself for thinking that.

"Oh, Benjamin. I've missed you. Will you not stay with us?"

"Where, Mother? Where are you? How can I stay? This is only a dream."

I sensed rather than heard the sound of my father's footsteps. He came up behind my mother and placed his hand on her arm. It was a courtly gesture. It struck me as wrong, somehow, like something that didn't fit his style.

"Ah, Ben. You're back, Son," my father said, smiling into my eyes. "How fortunate. Your mother has been beside herself. She feels guilty for leaving you."

I shook my head. These dreams were torturous. Why couldn't I wake up?

"Is he still fighting it?" my father asked my mother as if I'd suddenly disappeared.

She turned troubled eyes in my direction. Then she lifted a hand and laid it on my cheek. "Could you be happy here, Benjamin? It is very different, but I believe it is better."

I wanted to scream, to stop the dance and the music, to make everyone halt this façade of an alternate world. I opened my mouth as if I would do so, but my father suddenly clapped me on the back and said, "I'll teach you to hunt; I have a falcon. The horses are swift and full of spirit. And I, too, think you would be happy here, Ben. A dreamer like you would be much more successful here than in the old world."

"What are you talking about?" I blurted out, much louder than I meant to.

Several dancers looked our way, but no one stopped. They continued their slow-moving, courteous dance, lost in sophisticated refinement.

"Garland likes you," Mother said as if there weren't enough confusion already.

"What?"

"Garland, the dragon. She likes you," Mother explained as if clarifying the whole situation.

"There, that settles it," my father said. "Why don't you dance, Ben? See if you couldn't be happy with one of the fair, young lasses of the kingdom."

"Are you mad?" I snapped. "I don't have the foggiest idea how to dance like this," I said, waving my arm to indicate the groups of dancers. Even if I wanted to, this was just a dream, so it wouldn't make any difference. Besides, why would one of those girls want to dance with me? They don't even know me, and I must look odd."

Mother glanced down at my clothes. "Why, no," she said. "You look marvelous. Those clothes fit you well. You're quite handsome now — rather like your father, in fact," she added, giving him her usual warm smile.

Dad offered my mother his arm and said, "Shall we dance, Madam?"

She giggled like a schoolgirl and placed her hand on the broadest part of his well-muscled limb. But as they started to walk away, she turned back to look at me. "I can keep you here for about an hour, Benjamin. Try it out. See if it fits. We want you to be happy, dear. That's the most important thing. Be happy."

Dad was focused on his wife, but he pulled his fascination away from her long enough to glance at me. "Look, Ben, you don't seem to have much of a positive view of yourself, but here you're a good catch. Any of these maidens would be delighted to dance with you. Just don't make any moves on them. They have guardians." He laughed as they moved away, melding with the others, blending in perfectly.

I glanced over at the girl I'd been kind of keeping a watch on. She kept blushing every time I looked at her. She had a fan, like the other young girls, and each time I darted a peek, she raised it up to cover most of her face. When she wasn't hiding, I really liked what I saw.

Long chestnut hair falling to her hips, a tiny waist that showed off the fact that she was proportional in all the right places, eyes that held the lavender-blue of lupines, skin the color of powdered milk, and lips that. . . Let's just say that I was enthralled.

I walked toward her, trying to make eye contact. She fluttered the fan a bit more, but she looked bravely into my eyes. The lupines were sparkling like pale blue sequins. I couldn't have stopped my forward movement if an ogre had suddenly jumped in front of me. I was hooked, and all she needed to do was draw me in.

"Would you care to dance?" I asked, stealing my father's line.

The girl's eyes widened, and she curtseyed. "But, my lord," she said. "We haven't been introduced."

I was about to remedy that when a rather portly giant of a man stepped in between us. "How dare you address my charge," he growled at me. "Who are you?"

He was as fierce and as ugly as the ogre I was thinking about a minute ago. I backed up a step.

"Oh, don't be silly, Ferdinand," my goddess said. "He's the host's son — their only heir."

I was glad she'd interceded. For a moment, I wasn't sure what to say. After all, who was I in this dream world realm? I bowed to Ferdinand (and the lovely Helen of Troy look-alike) and said, "My name is Benjamin."

"He is so modest, Ferdinand. Listen to him. Lord Benjamin, I am honored to make your acquaintance. Now hush, Ferdinand, you can see he's quite safe."

Ferdinand still glared, but there was a light of recognition in his eyes that hadn't been there a moment before. Perhaps he was just slow to warm up to a person.

"The lady Serena has been gently reared, my lord. I watch her like the dragon beards its prey."

I had no idea what the dragon's beard had to do with dancing with Serena, but I nodded to him, put out my arm, as my father had, and was delighted to see the fair maiden place her gloved hand on my elbow. We exchanged smiles without her silly fan or her grouchy referee and began to weave our way into the dancing area.

I didn't plan on weaving too deeply, however. For one thing, I didn't want her glowering guardian to roar with anguish, and for another, I really had no idea how to do the dance everyone else was doing. As we walked forward, I quickly gave Serena my confession.

There was obviously no sense in putting it off; she'd discover my secret soon enough.

"I have been away at school," I said. "I've been too busy to learn to dance." Probably any school in the dream kingdom would have instructed me on the fine art of dancing, but Serena accepted my excuse and smiled even deeper into my eyes.

"You are so modest, my lord. I like that. It is obvious to me that you are as graceful as a silver unicorn and as elegant with words as a cultured elf.

The fact that she compared me with elves and unicorns made me a little uneasy. I hoped she wouldn't void her compliments after we'd danced. I concentrated even harder on not stepping on her feet.

Actually, the dance at the moment wasn't too hard to follow. It was quite different than the one I'd watched earlier. In this particular one, no partners were being exchanged. So Serena and I more or less rocked back and forth, skipped a couple of times, then clapped and turned about. It felt closer to an aerobics class for old ladies than any dance I'd ever seen.

The next dance was a slower, more formal dance. Our bodies never came in touch like they did in the real world. Here, hand upon hand, was about as close as a couple could come, and I'm not sure that even counted since Serena wore pale blue gloves that matched her velvet gown.

"How do you spend your time?" I questioned her, curious about not only a female's role in this society but also what her personal likes and dislikes might be.

"I work on tapestries mostly, my lord. The one I am weaving now is of a handsome unicorn sitting beside his friend, the dragon. My mother says it is not very realistic, but I like the concept. I believe that anything is possible. Are not unicorns and dragons both magical? Could they not be friends if they chose?"

I had no opinion about the matter. I knew next to nothing about either animal but I nodded that I agreed. Anything was possible.

"And you, my lord. How do you spend your days if I may be so bold to ask?"

I took a breath and thought. "I'm . . ."

I was saved by the interruption of the grumpy guardian. "You have taken up enough of the fair lady's time," he said. "It is not suitable for you two to dance another."

I hadn't noticed that the music had stopped. My hand was entwined with Serena's, and her eyes were still pouring her soul into mine.

Seeing that I was frozen in the moment, the guardian took Serena's hand from mine and walked her away. I just stood there watching. Serena's eyes held mine entrapped. I could tell she didn't want to leave.

"Good job," my father said as he walked by, my mother's hand still on his elbow. "That was a wise choice. Her father is a favored of the king's. It would be a good alliance."

"Now, Adam. You promised you wouldn't pressure him. He doesn't need to choose that quickly. Let him get used to it here. Take his time to see what he wants. We must allow him to make his own decisions," my mother scolded gently.

Dad never minded when my mother chided him. He picked up her hand and kissed it. "Yes, darling one. I shall back off, but I can't help praising my son when he shows wisdom now, can I?"

She returned his smile, her eyes glowing softly, her lips rounded into the "yes" of agreement.

I shook my head. Things were just too strange. I yearned to be back in bed again, safe and comfortable in my own world. I closed my eyes and concentrated. *Bed. House. Normality.*

But when I opened my eyes, my parents were still there, laughing at me a bit.

"It doesn't work like that, Benjamin," my mother said. "I've set the spells for you. You won't be going back until you fall asleep. And the next time you come, you'll be able to stay a few days. . ."

"Soon, she'll have you here full time," Dad interjected.

I stared at him, wondering if he was mad. Full time? Why would I want that? I'd end up in the insane asylum if that happened.

"Now, darling," Mom interrupted, placing her hand on my father's cheek. "Let him go dance now. Make merry, Benjamin. The whole night is yours."

Serena was dancing with another guy. I watched for a moment. Was her smile as big? Did she stare up at him with those heart-breaking lupine eyes as fascinated by his words as when she'd listened to mine?

"Ask another to dance, Benjamin. It is protocol. You must dance with all the young ladies."

"All?" I gasped.

Dad, seeing my expression, let out a chuckle. "Torture, right?" he laughed. "Go on. Your mother's right. It is your duty to please the young ladies. Be quick, and dance with them all. Then, if you still wish, you may ask the fairest for another round. But be careful. To mark one with favor is sometimes dangerous unless your intentions are carefully made known."

"Intentions?" I squawked. "You mean like marriage?"

"If it is your wish, Benjamin. But there's no hurry. You have all the time you'd like, and in the meantime, you will find every girl hopeful that you intend to choose her," my mother explained.

The night was young, and I learned to enjoy my *duty*. I discovered that adoring eyes came in many colors, and each of the faces held great beauty and grace. Amazingly, by the end of the ball, my dancing had also become quite proficient.

I did not ask the adorable Serena to dance again. I'd started my dancing too late. By the time I'd made my rounds, the guests were already leaving. But when Serena departed with her parents and guardian, her eyes once again connected with mine. My first choice was still my favorite. As I climbed up the long staircase, it was her face I was thinking of.

My bedroom was luxurious. The fireplace had been lit, and servants had placed hot water bottles in my bed to warm it comfortably. I dismissed the valet who'd come to undress me, tossed off the majority of my clothes, and slid into bed.

My parents came in to bid me goodnight. "Remember," my mother said. "We love you, Benjamin," and then she actually kissed me goodnight, something she hadn't done for many, many years.

My father nodded his head at me and said, "Hurry back to us, Ben. Next time you'll stay much longer. I'll take you hunting then, and we'll ride through the forest."

I smiled, but the heaviness of my eyes had entrapped me. The warmth of the hot water bottles against my body was urging me to sleep.

"Good night. I love you, too," I said as my eyes closed.

Chapter Twelve

I woke up in my own bed. I was not surprised. I'd expected it, but it still seemed odd after having bedded down in the suite of a castle. I could vaguely smell the scent of pine and smoke, yet there was no fireplace in my room. I sat up, half expecting to feel chilled bed bottles against my naked legs, but this bed had no such antiquated heating elements.

My feet hit the floor and pushed their way into the cozy house slippers I'd put there. Since I'd gotten my things from Pinecrest, I once again had something to wear that fit me correctly, but I still didn't have any idea about the nature of my day. I decided to eat breakfast first and then get dressed.

I stumbled into the kitchen to start up the coffee maker. I'd bought an expensive brand of coffee. The aroma filled the air, making me feel like a cartoon character, my nose riding the currents of the fragrance. I poured a glass of orange juice, took out the new loaf of bread, and shoved two slices into the toaster. That would start me off.

I sat down at the table and stared out the window. The birds were singing again. The sound made me happy, throwing me back into memories... When I was little, Dad and I took walks around the neighborhood. I used to own a little red wagon, and I'd set a stuffed animal inside and pull it along as we walked. Dad had been patient with me back then. He'd stopped and pointed out bird nests and imitated the sounds of the different birds. I still remember some of them. I knew how to duplicate the calls of blue jays, nightingales, turtledoves, and crows. We hadn't had the old owl who lived in the oak tree back then. The owl arrived much later, but there had always been robins' nests and the barn swallows that loved the eaves of our garage.

The toast popped up. I slathered it with margarine and dumped some marmalade on top. Then I carried the plate back to the table and sat there thinking about the past.

Dad looked happy in my dreams. He reminded me of what he used to look like before his face furrowed with worry lines. If it were possible, really possible, to do what my dreams suggested, would he have given up his law office? Would Mother? How could people change that much? How could . . .?

But that was silly. I bit into the toast and chewed. I wondered what they were eating in the castle right now. Did they have toast? Did they have coffee?

I poured myself a cup of the exotic coffee I'd bought, sweetened it with some sugar, and gave it a drop of milk. Heaven. How could my parents leave such a delightful drink behind?

As I was musing about the joys of drinking coffee, the old landline in the kitchen rang. I was expecting it to be the Gillicuttys, but it was Detective Smith.

"Any word from your parents?" she asked.

I thought about my dreams, took a sip of coffee, and swallowed. "No. I haven't found any useful clues. No papers, no letter to me or threatening letters, like you'd suggested to look for. Nothing."

The detective sighed into the phone. It sounded like she was writing down everything I told her. I hadn't said much yet it sounded like she was writing several lines. "I was afraid of that," she told me when she spoke again. The fingerprints came back from the bureau. Benjamin, no one was driving that vehicle except your father. The only other fingerprints found in the car were your mother's."

"Couldn't someone have been wearing gloves? Or maybe they wiped them off," I suggested, taking another sip of my brew.

The officer laughed. "No, Benjamin. No one wiped the car, and if there was someone in that car besides your parents, he or she wasn't driving. Your dad's fingerprints are all over that steering wheel."

"I see," I nodded my head as if she could see me. "Then we're back to the beginning. Where did they go? Why did they leave their car?"

Again, she sighed, a breathy little release of air that tickled my ear and made me think, for some reason, of a summer breeze. "I don't know, Benjamin. We're still looking, still asking people for any information they might have. We've been showing your parents' pictures to waitresses in restaurants and gas station clerks. Someone will recognize them. I'm sure of it."

The birds were still singing outside — louder than before. I'd never heard birds singing at Pinecrest. Too many kids, I guessed. Had the multitude of students kept any birds from sticking around?

"I hope someone knows something," I said, responding to the detective's words. "I hope my parents are okay. But it's been so long. . ."

"I know, Benjamin. I'm sorry. You okay?"

"Yes. The neighbors have been helpful. We're close. They've been driving me into town."

"Good. Take care of yourself, Benjamin. I'll be in touch."

I was still staring at the phone when the line went dead. I'd been expecting her to disconnect, but it still surprised me when it came. I'd wanted to ask her more questions. Funny thing — I didn't really have any.

I slipped the phone back on the receiver and sat down to finish my toast. My coffee was cold. I poured fresh. Then I thought about what I was going to do all day. The absence of plans didn't cheer me. Of course, I still had the key to test out, but I wasn't hoping for much there. I was sure now that my parents hadn't left me a note. They would have left it in the house. They would have made it easy for me to find if they'd wanted to give me a note. If they'd cared enough to do so . . .

I finished my coffee and returned to my bedroom to get dressed. No suit for me that day. I showered and slipped into comfortable jeans and a long sleeved navy polo. I pulled on some socks and slipped into and tied my black tennis shoes, checking them first for holes, as I always did. They were still okay but getting seedy, as my Mom would have put it. Time to order another pair.

My bed was a shambles from all the dreams of the night before. I pulled back the blankets and repositioned the top sheet, straightening and tucking it in at the end of the bed. I was just smoothing everything back into place when I saw a sudden sparkle of green. I gasped. Having been rather, unfortunately, close to Garland, I knew exactly what the thing was. I picked it up and turned it about. I was 100% positive that what I was holding was a dragon's feather. How could a dragon's feather have found its way into my bed — especially since there were no dragons — at least, not in this world?

I looked all about, including under the bed, but there was only the one feather I'd found. How had it gotten into my bed? And what was it really? I bit my lip, worrying over the question, and later had to put some salve on my lips because I'd made them bleed. It was only after I'd smeared my lips that I saw that a tiny drop of blood had fallen down onto the feather. I scrubbed it clean, but the blood stain remained. I applied soap and washed it again. Why was it still there? Blood shouldn't have stained it. How strange.

Chapter Thirteen

When the impossible slaps its paw on your knee, sometimes the only suitable response is to push it aside and not deal with it — at least, not at the moment. I placed that feather in the top drawer of my desk. It lay beside my erasers, a pack of gum, and three paper clips. In the darkness of the drawer, I could tell that it was glowing slightly, its light a beacon for my eyes, but I closed the drawer and turned away. I didn't want to think about dragon feathers. I couldn't.

The doorbell rang. I knew it was Harry coming to pick me up. We'd scheduled our meeting the day before. I made sure I had the new mystery key, pocketed my wallet, and grabbed the front door key.

"Coming," I called out.

I offered a cup of coffee to Harry, but he shook his head. "Just brushed my teeth. Are you ready?"

As I stepped out the door, a feather drifted down. I caught it. It was from the old owl who spent nights in the tree outside my window. Was that the feather I'd seen in my bed that morning? I wanted to go back to my room to compare. The oddness of the feather's glow, the one I'd found in my bed, had surely only been my imagination. For a moment, I was tempted. Then I saw Harry watching me.

"It's from the owl," I told him. "He first nested in that tree years ago. Dad said he had a mate then, but she died. Perhaps poisoned or hit by a car. The male must be getting pretty old now."

Harry cracked a smile at me. "The neighbors will sure be glad when he's gone. They're positive that old man is after their cats."

"A Western Screech Owl eats more insects than anything else," I laughed. "He probably sometimes dines on rats or mice, but a cat? That owl's just not big enough."

Not even a tasty bite would an owl make, said the air about me.

I looked up and around. I knew the voice wasn't Harry's. It sounded like. . . but it couldn't be . . .Yet, for a moment, I'd thought it was Garland, the dragon.

"You all right?" Harry asked. "You look pale?" Harry was giving me the same look he'd given me the night he found me out sleepwalking in my skivvies.

"I'm fine," I said. "Just not sleeping well yet. Let's go see if this key solves our mystery, shall we?"

Harry laughed as he slid into the front seat of his car. "I thought you didn't believe you'd find anything in the bank vault. Have you changed your mind?"

I climbed into the car, sitting beside Harry since Martha was once again home resting. I shook my head. "No. I doubt today's key will unlock any secrets, but we have to try everything."

He nodded as we backed out of the driveway and headed down the road. I was staring out the window. I thought I saw a rabbit hopping across the Bartlett's front yard. It looked like a tame one, a big white fluffy Easter bunny. I hoped a cat didn't get it, or the old owl. I started to mention it to Harry, but then I wasn't sure. Had I really seen the rabbit or just imagined it? Maybe it was like the dragon's feather or the voice I'd heard in my mind.

Thinking about that, the two of us rode in silence. I watched the houses of our neighbors, not as if I expected to see more rabbits or even birds digging for worms, but because I hadn't been around in a long while. I liked to see the changes, things like a new roof or a new tree planted in the front yard.

When we passed the Simon's place. I saw they had a little girl now. She was out riding her tricycle as her father dug in the rose garden. My parents hadn't told me of her birth. I wondered if they'd even noticed.

I like children, a voice said in my ear.

I jumped. Then I turned to look behind me. Of course, there was no one. Was I losing my mind? Was my parents' disappearance affecting me?

Harry said nothing, although he glanced at me, probably wondering about my sudden movement. Did he think I was acting strange?

"Detective Smith called," I told Harry, mainly so he wouldn't ask me if I was feeling all right again. "She says the police haven't found anything yet — except that the fingerprints on the steering wheel were my dad's. No one hijacked the car, in other words. Whatever happened, Dad was the one driving."

"Does she have any ideas?" Harry asked as he turned on the blinker, preparing to right turn into the bank's back parking.

I shook my head and tapped on the armrest. "No. It's like my folks just evaporated. They were there. People saw them. The truck driver even said he thought he saw someone behind the wheel. But he couldn't have, could he? Because they weren't there when the car hit the tree, and that was only seconds later.

"It doesn't make sense, Harry. Why would my parents have disappeared?" I complained for probably the hundredth time.

Harry parked under the shade tree and stopped the motor. "I don't know, Benjamin. I don't understand it either," he said, shaking his head slowly.

"You going to be okay in the bank? You want me to go in with you?"

I hadn't thought about Harry staying in the car. I'd just assumed he'd be at my side this time, but I didn't want to admit that, so I nodded my head. "I'll be fine, Harry. Thanks."

I headed for the entrance. Another feather dropped, this one sparkling in the sunshine. I reached up and grabbed it as it was falling. It was the same as the one in my bed.

"What's going on?" I whispered. "How can this be happening?"

I'm the spy for your parents, silly, the dragon said.

I whirled around, looking into the sky, but I couldn't see him. "Where are you?" I whispered, not wanting anyone who might be walking near us to hear me talking — apparently to myself.

You cannot see me. I am between the worlds.

"How can I hear you, then?"

For a dragon, it is easy to speak man talk. The words are merely scrambled. I sort them and send them back.

I'd stopped at the bottom of the bank's staircase. Harry was still sitting in the car reading his paper, but I knew he might look up at any minute. Then there would be questions.

I started up the steps. "You mean you speak into my mind, don't you?" I said.

The dragon laughed. Instinctively, I looked about, checking to see if anyone else could hear.

No one else can hear me, Benjamin.

"Good. Don't talk now. I have to concentrate," I said as I opened up the huge glass door of the bank.

The smell of formaldehyde assaulted me. The bank had just put in a new carpet. I covered my nose and walked over to the customer assistance section.

"Yes, may I help you?" a middle-aged woman with a brown mole on her lip asked.

I looked away to avoid staring. "Does this key open a safe deposit box?" I asked, handing her the newest mystery key.

"Why, yes. This is one of ours. Where did you get it?"

That brought my eyes up. She was looking at me as if I'd stolen it. Her dress had large orange flowers on it. I wondered if she was Hawaiian.

"It's my parents' key. I need to see their box," I told her, staring at the flowers so I didn't look at her mole.

"Do you have a letter from them giving you permission to enter?"

I was attempting to answer that when the bank manager came over, apparently having spotted me while the flower lady was probing.

"Ah, Benjamin Thorne. How are you today? Any word yet?"

He'd thrust out his hand as if I were an adult. I felt honored.

"No. No word, I'm afraid. I found a key in my father's safe. May I see if there's anything in their box?" I asked.

"Why, of course, Benjamin. Mrs. Clune, please assist Mr. Thorne. He's a good client of ours. Give him anything he needs."

Mrs. Clune looked surly about that, but she nodded. I signed in on the line she pointed to and then passed through a small wooden gate.

It felt like I was entering some kind of secret club. I expected her to ask me for the password, but we just slipped through the metal doorway and into the realm of the inner vault. I'd never been inside. The rows and rows of boxes, all bearing numbers, were impressive.

We found my parents' box, a rather large one at the bottom. Using my key and the one that belonged to the bank, Mrs. Clune unlocked the box, slid it out of position, and handed it to me. Then she led me to a small room, told me to take my time, and shut the door.

I pried back the lid of the metal box. There were lots of papers inside and the small wrapped package containing the necklace my father had planned to give my mother. I looked at it, and the note scribbled in his hand that told her how much he loved her. I placed the note back in the box and set it down on the counter.

I went through the papers, one by one — more copies of the will, which I decided to read just in case it would tell me something new. I learned very little. I was to inherit everything, but if I died before that time, Martha and Harry Gillicutty were next in line. I wondered if they knew about the will. I looked down at the bottom, where the signatures of the witnesses were. I'd never heard of the first witness of the document, but the second signature belonged to the bank president.

I folded the will back into its holder and returned it to the box. Then, I read through the other papers. They were only property deeds, stock certificates, and legal documents that I didn't bother to investigate. There was nothing addressed to me and not one thing that gave me a single clue about where my parents might have gone.

Chapter Fourteen

I thanked Mrs. Clune, nodded to the bank president, and walked toward the door. I knew Harry would be waiting for me. Besides, what else could I accomplish in a bank except to take out money that I didn't need yet?

On the way down to the stairs, Garland spoke to me. *Why did you spend time in that ugly building? Forests are the places for agreeable thoughts.*

I almost missed a step, almost tumbled down the staircase, but I caught myself and held onto the rail. Carefully, I continued down. I didn't bother looking around. I knew I wouldn't see the dragon. *You're my imagination, Garland. You're not real. Why should I talk to you?*

I didn't say the words out loud, of course. I merely thought about them, rationalizing with myself because, indeed, I'd begun to believe that I might be going crazy.

The response came swiftly. Obviously thought travels instantaneously when one converses with a dragon or with one's self.

Imagination? Garland said. *How lovely. I am well content to be inside your mind. But why do you say I'm not real?*

I stopped to mop my brow. I glanced at the tree standing guard over Harry's car. A vibrant-colored bird was sitting on a limb, at least I thought so at first, but when I blinked, the bird was gone. Imagination again. *I'm not going to talk to you. This is insanity,* I whispered to myself.

I reached the foot of the stairs. Harry was still engaged in the reading of his newspaper. I paused to untangle my brain, my eyes once again searching the tree, looking for something that could have given me the illusion of a multi-colored bird . . .

Go away, I told the dragon, gritting my teeth as I thought the words. *There are no dragons. Not in this world, anyway.*

How droll," he laughed. *Yet I am here, and I do exist, as my stomach will tell you. Where do you keep your wild deer? I have seen only cars. Where am I supposed to hunt? A goat would do, I suppose, or a nice fat . . .*

You can't hunt here. There aren't any animals. Leave me alone, I almost shouted out. I was only saved from vocalizing the words by a passing bank customer who walked up the stairs on the other side of me.

I am in your world because I promised your parents I'd watch over you. When I see you back to your uncastle-like dwelling, I shall have to find something to eat. It is not safe for a dragon to become too hungry. We . . .

Go home, then. You can hunt there. Harry, as if feeling my presence, laid down his newspaper and waved to me. I waved back. I didn't know what else to say to the dragon anyway... How could you argue with something that couldn't be real?

I opened the door of Harry's car and slid in. "I didn't find anything in the safe security box," I said. "There was nothing there but a necklace and some legal stuff. Oh, and my parents' wills. I glanced through them."

"I imagine your parents left everything to you, didn't they?" Harry said as he backed out of the parking spot.

"Yes." Should I tell him what I'd read? Should I mention what would happen if I died? Or did Harry already know?

"Did my parents ever talk to you about their wills?" I probed, watching him as if I thought he'd suddenly look furtive.

Harry turned on the blinker, glanced at me, and asked, "Now, why would your parents consult me, Benjamin? I'm an old man. I don't know anything about legal stuff. That's their department. I do know that Martha and I weren't asked to be witnesses for them. But I figured your parents had lots of people willing to do that. I paid it no mind."

I sighed. Harry probably didn't know then. It was like my parents to go do something like that and not discuss it with anyone. Who else would they have given their money to? They had no relatives. Neither of them felt strongly about their alma maters. Nor were they churchgoers. And although they gave to charities, they weren't strong believers in that area either. I guess giving it to their neighbors made as much sense as anything else. Harry and Martha had spent a lot of time with me. They were my family, even if not my parents' family.

I leaned back against the seat, thinking about it. "Yeah, that's what I figured, Harry. They used the bank president and someone I've never heard of as their witnesses."

"Maybe the other person is someone in their offices or a personal friend," Harry said, although he acted as if he wasn't the least curious. I think he was just allowing me to talk.

"Yeah, I guess so." I sighed and stretched out my leg. The gesture reminded me of Harry and how his knees always hurt him, which made me recall how Dad used to say that if Harry exercised regularly, he wouldn't have so much pain. But Dad was an attorney, not a doctor. What did he know about aging knees? And that reminded me of my dreams, dreams where he was wearing violet tights and funny-looking pointed toes.

"What am I going to do, Harry? I'm out of clues now."

Harry had stopped at a red light. He stretched out his hand and patted mine, "There's nothing you can do, Benjamin. Sometimes you just got to hand your problems over to the good Lord and let Him solve them."

I sighed, even heavier than before. Harry and Martha were Baptists. They went dependably every Sunday. It was easy for them to say things like that. They were always telling me to trust in the Lord, but I hadn't been raised in their faith. I hadn't been raised in any faith. Frankly, I found such things hard to believe, but I didn't say anything. I just watched the road as Harry continued driving.

Martha had prepared lunch for us. We sat down and feasted on tuna sandwiches with pickles and chopped celery (just the way I liked them), potato salad, and chocolate cake for dessert.

"I thought you were supposed to be resting while we were gone," I commented, worried, even as I chewed and swallowed.

Martha laughed. "Oh, you men! Now I've got two of you stewing over my welfare." She giggled. "Well, if you must know, Harry's the one who made the cake. He even iced it. And he put together the potato salad last night while I was watching a game show on the TV."

"You were the one who put the potatoes on to boil," he added, grinning.

She ignored him and swatted a fly that had come in through the front door. Her aim was good. She scooped it up and threw its carcass into the trash.

"Don't be silly, now you two. All I did was mix the tuna salad while you were off having your adventure. Now, tell me — what did you find in the safe security box, Benjamin? I'm desperate to hear."

There wasn't much to tell. The look on Martha's face reflected exactly the way I felt. Mysteries weren't supposed to go unsolved. They were supposed to leave breadcrumbs so you could follow them.

Seeing my expression and the way Martha looked made Harry hop in with the latest town gossip. "I bet you two don't know about the new restaurant opening up over on Wilshire Avenue."

Martha and I looked at each other. A new restaurant? For some reason, that started us all laughing. The meal continued pleasantly after that. We were soon talking about what kind of food they'd have and about the weather, and then, whether there'd be zucchini in another week.

I told them how I wanted to find out if there was still a job for me at my father's office. They turned silent and looked at me. I explained about how Dad had set it up.

After we'd cleaned up, with the Gillicuttys' encouragement, I even dialed the number of Dad's Law firm and asked to speak to Mr. Dougherty, the second in command.

At first the man had lots of questions about what I'd heard from the police concerning my parents, but after I told him, the silence came, and I had to tread through muddy water. I was just about to jump in when Mr. Dougherty asked me about my college plans. So I told him how I'd be going to Chatsworth University, just like my dad.

"Fine school," Mr. Dougherty commented.

I could hear the minutes ticking away on the clock in the kitchen. The Gillicuttys' eyes were on me, too. I had to get this over with. I had to ask. I dashed in the moment Mr. Dougherty stopped telling me about his college experiences at UCLA.

"Mr. Dougherty, my dad, before the crash and all, said there might be a job for me at the law office this summer. Do you think that's still possible . . . ? I mean, with everything that's happened and all. . ."

The pause was only a second before Mr. Dougherty smoothly answered. "Why, sure, Benjamin. We can find something for you to do. We're always happy to find an eager worker to run things over to the courthouse or do our gopher work. When do you want to start?"

I didn't know what gopher work was, but I was willing to learn. I suggested that the next day would be fine, and it was agreed upon. Mr. Dougherty told me to come to his office at 8:30, and I said I would. Then, with nothing left to be said, we gave our goodbyes.

"I've got a job," I said, turning around to smile at the Gillicuttys. Martha clapped her hands. "We're so proud of you, Benjamin," she told me. The light in Harry's eyes told me he felt the same.

It would be my first job. I felt rather nervous about that, but with the offering of a second piece of chocolate cake, my worry receded — at least temporarily.

Chapter Fifteen

In my dream that night, the countryside we were pounding through consisted of one long, dirt and dust-filled trail hemmed in on both sides by trees that had the look of cherry, walnut, fig, and a few sparse patches of pecan. Nowhere did I see anything wild – like oaks, maples, or birch. This acreage produced food.

We had been galloping up and down fair-sized hills for over an hour when I began to wonder about our steeds. Mine had little sweat, and his breath was still even and steady. I thought back to my days of horsemanship school. Such a thing wasn't possible for those horses. We students had been cautioned to gallop only for short periods and then to pull them up for breathers, which meant walking a bit, or at least only trotting slowly.

The sun was sharply overhead. The day had heated. I let go of my saddle horn with one hand and shrugged out of my jacket. I noticed that others had done the same. Most of the men were already stripped down, a few even going bare-chested.

My father had remained at my side. He saw my gaze and smiled. "This is the way life should be, isn't it, Benjamin?"

I could see, even without his words, that he was enjoying this mad gallop, but I was uncomfortable. My thighs ached. I kept shifting in the saddle, seeking a more comfortable position.

I will gladly carry you, Garland said from overhead. I looked up and saw her. Her great wings were floating just below the clouds.

"Gripped in your claws? I tried that. You almost dropped me," I told her.

My father thought I was replying to him. "What?" he shouted, but then he saw the sparkling green of the dragon's wing. "Ah," he said. "Your mother has sent the dragon. Good. That will impress the King."

Garland had obviously been affronted by my words. He zoomed down low, soared over the heads of the horses, and plucked me off mine. I barely disconnected from the stirrups in time, leaving my horse with an awkwardness that made the animal start, shy to the side, and then bolt.

"No!" I cried out, but it was too late. Disconnected from the stirrups, the wind caught my yell and carried it in an updraft that erased it from everyone's hearing. Only my father must have perceived my voice as dismayed, angry, and full of panic.

And how did he react to it? He laughed. "Ah, to be young again," I heard him shout.

If I'd had a fist, I might have disrespectfully waved it in his face, but I was rather occupied at the time, fighting against the dragon claws that were pushing me up against her loudly beating chest, half smothering me in downy green feathers.

"I told you not to do that," I said, spitting out a feather that had intruded, uninvited, into my mouth.

"Words cannot show. Not for a human. I am proving that I would not drop you."

"Okay, I believe you, but you're smothering me in feathers. Can't you loosen your grasp slightly?"

"You will not be afraid?"

We were twenty feet up in the air. We'd long ago passed the horses and were climbing above the clouds. If I'd been enclosed in a metal construction of nuts and bolts, I'd have had no fear, but being clutched in a dragon's grasp was a little overwhelming.

So I lied. "No, not scared at all. Now, can you take me back to my horse?"

Garland let out a giant puff of smoke and flame. "Never lie to a dragon," she told me. "Never."

The heat from her breath was welcome. The air up high was frigid, but the reminder that she was a real dragon and fully capable of searing my skin into charred hamburger did not in any way lessen my fear. My heart, already galloping faster than the horses had, suddenly took off for the moon.

"Rest easy, Benjie," the dragon soothed. "I will not turn you into charred anything. You are my chosen one. I shall protect you. I shall always keep you safe."

Chapter Sixteen

When she finally allowed me to breathe more freely, I realized that Garland smelled not of feathers but of cooked coconuts. It was a pleasant odor. I told her so, and she chuckled deep in her chest.

"Tell me if you get cold, my little Benjie," she said. "I can warm you a bit by blowing out hot air if you like."

I was almost eighteen years old, a former swimming champion, a darn good soccer player, and soon to be an employed college student. I was NOT someone's LITTLE Benjie. Of course, I expelled that thought in an outpouring of indignant objections.

Again, I heard Garland's deep-chested chuckle as she laughed at me. My face heated, and I snapped, "You can put me down NOW."

She ignored my demand, as she seemed to ignore most of what I asked her to do. "Benjie, I didn't mean that you were a child, exactly, although, in dragon years, you are scarcely out of the egg. I only meant that your body is small — again, in comparison to my species, not yours."

Okay. That placated me a bit. I sighed, and my anger lessened. "Okay, sorry. But don't refer to me as your little Benjie again."

Once more, the dragon chuckled. "I don't recall hearing any outrage on your part when Serena called you that."

I didn't comment. There were just some things one can't explain — especially not to a warm, feathery dragon, especially one holding me up in the sky at more or less jet altitude.

I changed the subject and asked Garland something I'd been curious about. "I thought dragons were reptiles. Why do you have feathers?"

Gracefully, Garland followed my lead and began to expound on how dragons were not really reptiles but semi-rare magical beasts, more closely related to eagles and hawks.

Garland's snout did not look like a bird's beak. It resembled a crocodile's huge, toothy, cavernous mouth, but I thought of the pelican. A bird that had an equally large-sized oral cavity. I figured that maybe Dragons had evolved from a distant relative of theirs.

"We do not share ancestors with the pelican," Garland assured me haughtily, although I had not mentioned my musings.

It was time for another change in the subject matter. "Were there ever dragons in my world?" I asked.

That immediately cheered Garland. She boomed with enthusiasm, "No, not in your world. Magic is only half-formed there. It comes out flawed and imperfect. Oh, we can visit occasionally, and we do periodically check on things, but we never stay there. That world is boring, tasteless, and hugely over-crowded. Even unicorns dislike the place, and they usually like everywhere. Unicorns, you see, are the optimists of the universe."

That was all very interesting, and I had a great many questions to ask Garland about the universe and unicorns, but at that moment, for some strange reason, I remembered I was supposed to be rising early and starting the long bike ride to my first day of work.

What if being in this world made me late? What if I completely missed my first day of work? What if I were fired before I even started?

"I have to speak to my father," I told the dragon. "Right now. It's important."

"But we haven't reached the King's castle yet. The others are still far behind us."

I didn't understand what that had to do with anything. I wiggled, deeply concerned over the urgency of my situation, hoping that for once Garland wouldn't argue and would return me to my father's side.

She sighed. "You agonize needlessly about such things. Your father has no power, anyway. It is your mother who guides the transitions. Besides, if you got fired, then you could stay here. This is the better place for you."

She was still arguing, but I noticed that she'd wheeled us about and was returning me back to my father.

"Thank you," I told her. "It is very important to me that I don't get fired."

I know, Garland whispered into my mind. "I can feel your wishes, Benjamin. A dragon always knows what his person most desires. A human's will is much stronger than mere words."

Chapter Seventeen

Garland dropped me off right next to my father. The whole troop was resting by the side of the road. If they thought being delivered by a dragon was slightly odd, their faces didn't reflect it. Even the blue complexions of the strange ones showed not the least reaction.

"Did you have a pleasant flight?" Dad asked like I'd gone hang gliding or something.

I nodded. The others were all listening, and besides, the only thing I wanted to talk about was how I was going to get back to *my* universe before it was time to go to work. I didn't know if I should talk about such things in front of them.

I sat down beside my father and began a whispered explanation. At first, he beamed and patted me. That was at the part where I explained about calling Mr. Dougherty. But when I told him how I was supposed to start the job in the morning and how I was planning to ride his bike, Dad held up his hand and stopped my words.

"Absolutely not," he said. "I don't mind your using the bike. Everything is yours now, Benjamin — all the money, the house, the properties. Your mother and I can never go back. But I absolutely forbid you to ride that bike clear into town. That is too dangerous."

The leader of the group declared the rest period over. Dad bolted up as if our conversation were over. He put his hand behind my back and pushed me toward the horse I'd previously been riding. When the beast saw me, its ears went back, almost touching its head. It retracted two ugly gray lips and bit at the air in warning.

I backtracked just as it lashed out with a back hoof that came alarmingly close to a rather delicate part of my midsection.

"Ah, Dad, I think . . ."

"Yeah," he laughed. "Looks like he doesn't like your dragon smell. The odor never bothered me, but I've heard that some animals refuse to carry a dragon rider. I guess this one is making it pretty clear he opposes the idea. Maybe you just better climb up on Garland and forget about rejoining our group."

"But what about my first day at work? I can't be late."

My father shook his head. "Forget about it. Your mother's in charge of that. If she wants you back in time, she'll send you there. Otherwise, it's out of your control."

So saying, Dad strode over to his horse, climbed aboard, and bellowed with all the others the particular chant, which apparently meant, "Gallop on."

I stepped out of their way and watched as the whole group practically stampeded on down the road.

"Good," Garland said. "This will give us ample time to teach you how to ride dragon back."

The dragon, now that the horses were gone, had alit in the middle of the road. Folding her wings at her side, she bugled up at the sun.

"What was that for?" I asked, jumping slightly at the sound of it.

Her mouth opened, and again, she pierced the air with the horrid scream. "I am announcing," she told me calmly.

The sun was shining on her green-feathered hide. Her feathers seemed to collect the rays, for as I watched, they turned into a thousand mirrors of light. I looked away, longing for a good pair of sunglasses.

I heard a roar from the sky and then another from the other side. I looked up and saw dragons coming — a sky full of them.

I had begun to trust Garland. After all, my mother and father had confidence that she wouldn't eat me, but a flock of dragons (or whatever you call an entire group of them) was totally different. I turned at the waist, rotated my knees and feet, and took off running.

"Benjamin, stop!" Garland bleated, but I kept going. Whether I was dreaming or not, I knew that dragons had fiery breaths, teeth like ice picks, and claws that could rip and tear. Who was it that once said, "Discretion is the most important part of valor?"

Maybe I didn't quite get that right, but I was sure that whoever had said it was probably still alive, while I bet a person hunted by dragons never grew gray hair.

I was speeding between trees, really going faster than I'd ever run on the sprint tests at school when my shirt was suddenly seized in a vice of teeth against teeth. I spun my heels, going nowhere.

You will not run from me, my chosen one, Garland, snarled into my mind, using such force it was like a whip of anger, one that started off another huge headache.

I sucked in my breath and turned to face her — at least I tried. Her teeth were still gripping the back of my shirt.

I shouldn't have looked. If you've never seen an angry dragon's eyes, which turn red and then rotate faster than emergency beacon lights, you are lucky. Once seen, I promise you'll never forget.

Garland's former gentle manner had been completely replaced with that of a furious and frightening monster. I fought her grip on me, then started unbuttoning, ready to take off the moment I was free.

"Don't you dare," she blared at me. "My next bite might be skin."

I froze. I couldn't bear to look at her, then, and I didn't dare move. I was trembling, petrified with terror, but the thing that hit me hardest at that moment was my urgent need to empty my bladder.

Garland let go. "Humans! Have you no sense at all? Water the ground and be fast about it. The whole Dragon's Weyr has come to observe you, and so far, you've been a considerable disappointment to them."

Disappointment? I was on the brink of wetting myself. The thought of being a Dragon Weyr's disappointment seemed far less important.

I'd have preferred to have some privacy, but at the sight of Garland's eyes, all arguments were squelched. I slid my pants down, urinated over a large mushroom, and fastened up as quickly as possible — which wasn't easy since my fingers were shaking so badly they barely functioned, and my costume had four buttons about the crouch.

When I turned around, Garland's eyes had simmered down to only streaks of red. Their movement had slowed, too. I took a deep breath. "I'm sorry I panicked," I said. "I thought they'd come to . . ."

"I must remember you have no training in dragon lore," Garland sighed. "I suppose you're not even aware of the fact that most dragons would never eat a sentient being."

No, that was one of the things they'd never taught me at school. I was glad to hear it, although I wondered how I could recognize the dragons who didn't observe such high moral standards.

Garland laughed. "You really are amusing, my pet."

I opened my mouth to comment on her descriptor, but I shut it without saying a word. Then I followed Garland back to the road, still feeling timid about meeting a Weyr of Dragons.

Chapter Eighteen

I felt like I was the only player on a huge football field; all around me, eyes were staring down from sky-high bleachers. The sun was still at full beam, and the feathers of the dragons shone in a variety of hues: brownish-bronze, aquamarine, orangish-melon, lemon-yellow, and the many shades of green, like Garland. Greens outnumbered the others by far.

Again, I wished for dark glasses. The sparkling reflections of their feathers burned my eyes. I shaded my brow for a moment with the palm of my hand. Then I tried shutting my eyes, hoping to avoid the glare completely. That worked for a moment, but then a dragon called out to me questioningly, and I looked up to see which one was speaking.

"Have you made your decision to stay yet?" a blue-green dragon, the largest of those present, queried me.

I drew in a breath, ready to answer, but Garland spoke first. "I told you he is new to this world. He doesn't accept it yet. He hasn't even met the King."

"Not met the King? Why not?" several said at the same time.

"I am supposed to be on my way there now," I answered, my eyes once again scanning faces, colors, and moods.

"I will stay with him no matter his choice," Garland stated, her clawed hand (paw?) touching my shoulder lightly.

But that cannot be," several bellowed. "Where is the precedent?"

The aquamarine dragon lowered into the middle of the road. I would have backtracked away from its arrival had Garland's hand not prevented that. Her claws dug deep, warningly. Understanding the admonishment, I didn't move. I stood tall, pretending to be brave. The huge one stepped closer and lowered its head so it could peer into my eyes.

"She tells me that you smell nice," the great one said.

I shrugged. I didn't know.

"Garland also says that she chose you because she likes your mind. You amuse her. Will that last?"

The huge dragon smelled of summer barbecues or autumn leaves. It was a scent that took me back in time to when my father used to cook hot dogs over the grill. I inhaled and held it.

But those times were gone. Perhaps I needed to let them go. Perhaps I needed to . . .

"What is it you need, small human? Normality?"

That wasn't at all what I'd been thinking, but yet when the dragon said the word, it clicked. Maybe I did want normality. It had certainly been a very long time since I'd had any.

"I smell possibilities in him, Garland. He could become what you envision, but there is still the question in him. He is unsettled. All right. We shall wave the ceremony for now. Stay with him, guard him, but do not force him to commit. He is not ready. He may never be."

The dragon gave me his name as, Foster. I knew enough to feel honored. I bowed to him, then watched him soar up into the sky. He circled once, then flew off toward the east. One by one, the Weyr followed. In a moment, only Garland remained, still silent, one claw firmly attached to my shoulder.

"We must go now," she said. "Climb up. I shall take you to meet the King."

"You need to tell me what that was about. What ceremony, Garland? What does it mean?"

"Hurry, Benjamin. The hour grows late. We must make haste to arrive at the moment the others do."

Garland's legs were rough-hued scales. I climbed her front right, pulling myself up with a firm grip on her feathers.

"That doesn't hurt you?" I asked again.

She chuckled deep in her chest; a sound I was learning meant that everything was fine.

I positioned myself with my legs spread out, clutching the feathers on the lower part of her neck. Then she lifted up and soared into the sky, flapping her wings strongly, heading toward the west.

Once we were in the sky, I tried asking my questions again, but although she answered them, each answer came with another puzzle.

"Why did the Weyr come to meet me?" I queried.

"It is a rule," she replied.

"What rule?"

Her body vibrated with amusement.

"Look, I know you think my questions are ridiculous, but couldn't you help me out a little? You know I don't understand this world. Can't you give me a base of knowledge, tell me what's going on — what the rules are, tell me about the Weyr and about the king I'm supposed to meet?"

Her breath hit me in the face with warmth and sweetness and coated with a bit of laughter. "You are right, Benjamin. It must be difficult to understand. I feel your frustration, but you must find a way. You must build your own path of knowledge. No one can do that for you."

Circles of perplexity — maybe that's how the dream world always works. I closed my mouth and started thinking, searching for bridges between what I knew and everything that puzzled me.

Chapter Nineteen

Garland flew steadily against the wind. I could tell she was growing tired. I kept asking her if she didn't need to rest, but she kept on, only occasionally sending puffs back to warm me when she felt me shivering from the cold.

The sun had sunk between two mountain peaks. Roses had tinted the sky with smeared petals of pink, then slathered marmalade and butter around the edges before the King's castle came into sight. And there, on the road toward the great drawbridge, rode my father and the other men.

"There they are," I cried out, but Garland had already seen them. She circled lower, spiraling toward a point of contact with the troop, one right at the entrance across the moat.

As we lowered, I made out my father riding straight and tall in the saddle. It was rather a shock to see how well he blended in with the other riders. He looked nothing like the sophisticated lawyer he'd been two weeks before.

Then it hit me. It couldn't have been only weeks before. Too much had changed with Mom and him. They'd adapted to this alien world, for one thing. How much time had that taken?

"Time doesn't keep pace here with my world, does it, Garland?"

At first, I thought she'd ignore my question, but as we touched down, she turned her head and cocked it in a manner that told me I'd amused her again. "Your concept of time is like the ants that crawl about in the soil," she told me. "Do all of them follow the same path?"

I took that as a "I'd guessed right." I wondered how long my parents had lived in this kingdom according to this other world's time frame.

I started to ask the dragon, but my father had just dismounted and was walking toward me. I slipped off Garland and met him halfway.

"Everything okay?" he asked, looking me up and down as if I might have a broken arm or two.

I nodded. "What does the King want to see me for, Dad? You never explained that."

My father's eyes scanned my face, then looked back at the others. "No time to explain, son. The King is holding off dinner for our arrival. We dare not dally."

Dally? Since when had Dad spoken like someone out of another century? What had happened to erase his legal talk?

As Dad and I stepped onto the plank of the moat crossing, I turned back to speak to Garland. "Aren't you coming with us?" I asked.

She rumbled her usual chuckle, opened up her mouth, and breathed out a fierce bellyful of fire and laughter. Then she tilted her head to stare at me. "Benjamin, I shall wait where dragons wait. Inside your human habitats, there are only small walls and narrow halls. Outside is better. But I am linked to you. I shall always know your need."

My father's hand on my back was pushing me forward. I didn't stop to argue. Besides, when had I ever argued with my father? I sighed heavily and listened to the sound of the troop of men behind us.

Next to my father was one of the blue, three-limbed ones. I studied him as we walked. My father, noticing my interest, introduced me. "This is Kefthar," he said. "Kefthar, this is my son, Benjamin."

Kefthar took his fist and slammed it into his head. "Lord Benjamin, welcome," he said.

I had no intention of striking myself with a fist. I merely nodded and thanked him.

My father and I smiled at each other, so I guess what I'd done was adequate. Being in a strange land meant that I never knew when I'd step in a pile of something objectionable — not that I was an expert in my home world, either. I was remembering the upcoming first day on the job. Would I know what to do in a legal office? Wasn't that rather like heading into a strange land?

And when would my first day on the job happen, I wondered for the twentieth time.

"I saw that you are a skilled dragon rider," Kefthar said. "That is good."

It took a moment for me to realize he was referring to my ride on Garland. *Me, a skilled dragon rider?* I started to explain that it was my first time riding a dragon, but my father interrupted.

"My son is humble. He doesn't realize how many skills he possesses. I am very proud of him, Kefthar. It is good he is here with us."

In all my years, I never once remembered my father praising me. It threw me into speechless mode. I gaped like a fish thrown onto land.

We entered through heavy wooden gates. As I watched, blue men closed them behind us. The hinges seemed made of iron. They squeaked. Didn't the king know they were rusting?

Inside, we continued down a path of wooden planking; the horses' heavy tread made a slow clop-clop sound that pounded my brain. I closed my eyes a moment and massaged my head.

"What's the matter, Benjamin? Does your head hurt?"

To tell anything but the truth would have served no purpose. My pain was growing bolder. I was sure that I'd soon pass out if it continued to escalate.

"He's got a headache?" Kefthar bellowed. "I can fix that with a whiz and a shake."

Before either my father or I had a chance to ask what a whiz and a shake was, Kefthar lifted me up into the air, turned me upside down, and swung me back and forth. It must have panicked my brain into behaving because when the huge blue man was finished and he set me back down on my feet, the pain had completely disappeared.

My father and Kefthar laughed, then clapped each other on the back. I said nothing. Sometimes, that's the best thing to do when life turns you upside down and swings away every single thing that makes sense.

Chapter Twenty

We passed dozens of blue-skinned guards, all of them decked out with bands of leather straps that crisscrossed tightly over their chests. Their costume reminded me of Mexican banditos. However, their purple tights kind of confused the picture. Their satin lavender vests hinted at a totally different image.

The guards' bands were arrayed with vicious, sharp-edged knives that formed elaborate, horizontal patterns. Each of the guards' three elongated arms held even more fierce-looking weapons — swords, epees, and something that looked like a live, stiff-limbed octopus.

I shuddered each time we passed another set of them. They watched us intently as we continued down the long, narrow halls of the inner courtyard.

Shouldn't we have come to a room? Wasn't there supposed to be a reception hall or something?

I glanced behind to see if the company of men was still following us, although I knew from the sound of their feet on the hard packed dirt that they were. What I hadn't realized was that the men were still leading the horses, even though we must be deep inside the castle walls. Why hadn't we come to the stables yet, or at least split apart so the animals could be groomed and bedded down?

As if that thought had just registered on the castle's architect, we arrived at an intersection. It opened out into a large open courtyard, one with trees and bushes, grass, and even a small fountain.

The horses neighed as they smelled water. They pulled against the men's hold, eager to drink. One by one, they were taken to the fountain. Unlike real horses, these turned their head to the side and gurgled the water up noisily. I was so fascinated by their manner of drinking that I didn't notice my father had kept going.

"Benjamin, come on," he shouted back at me. "The King is waiting."

The loud reminder drew the eyes of the others. They studied me openly, curiously, as if I'd suddenly sprouted horns.

I caught up with my father without running, but I was embarrassed. I knew they'd heard the scolding note in my father's voice. Even the guards standing at the entrance to the hall fastened scornful eyes on me. I wished I could hide.

He feels great love for you, Benjie. You have done nothing for which he is ashamed; Garland's voice sounded in my ear, making me jump right in front of one of the scornful-eyed guards.

Instinctively, since I'd surprised him, I suppose, the guard did a quick step with his feet, lowered the arm that held his sword, and sent its sharp point inches from my chest.

As quickly, he dropped the spear, and it thudded as it hit dirt. But I was caught with my mouth open, frozen as a stone statue.

"Benjamin, now what's wrong?" my father barked, turning around to check my whereabouts.

Obviously, my father hadn't seen the guard's attack. Dad probably hadn't even noticed that I'd just been transposed into a petrified top half with wilting, shaky legs. It was logical to assume that my father also didn't see the three-limbed blue-skinned guard groveling on the ground, his face only a hand's width from my foot, for my father bellowed out, "Son, I know this is all new to you, but you really must keep up."

I stepped over the guard's arms, flung grovel-style across my path, picked up the fallen sword, inserted it back into the man's hand, and trotted after my father.

We were soon winding in and out of corridors, following the path that changed from hard-packed dirt to uneven stone walkways. I noticed tapestries on the wall, tapestries that carried some kind of phosphorous growth that lighted our way forward. It was a good thing they had that because I could see no other lighting system, and as we walked deeper into the middle of what seemed an enormous structure, it grew darker and darker.

We arrived at a hexagon-shaped junction where the phosphorous glowed even brighter. Six guards stood with their backs stiff against the wall, in positions that were supposed to prevent our continuing down the path.

"State your purpose," one of the burly blues demanded, letting his octopus weapon slide into a more battle-accessible position.

That didn't faze either my father or Kefthar. They hardly paused, heading straight for the octopus, which, by the way, had elongated its arms and was making a raspy, coughing noise rather like that of a sick vacuum cleaner.

I kept my eye on the thing, completely distrustful of both its vibrating gargle and the ends of its tentacles, which looked like they might carry potent stingers. My father, however, was not cautious about it at all. He stepped closer and held his hand over the fat head part. "I am, Baron Adam Thorne, here by the command of my King," he intoned with the same voice he always used in court when he was giving his closing statements.

Then, his words echoed across my brain. My father was a Baron? Wasn't that some kind of nobility? When had that happened?

"I have brought my son as requested. If His Majesty allows, I would like to present Lord Benjamin."

The octopus thing had to be some kind of intercom, yet it was obviously wireless. It did not reply to my father's words, yet the guard holding it stepped back, and Kefthar moved into position, placing his hand directly on the thing's spiny-looking head. He began to talk, too, but I couldn't understand a word he said. I hoped the King understood Blue Speech.

From the corner of my eye, I saw someone spring forward. I wheeled around as if I expected another attack. But this time, it wasn't one of the guards mistaking me for a bad guy; it was a young girl.

I stared at her just as intently as she was watching me. Four long carrot-colored braids hung down at the side of her thin, brown-freckled face. She had streaks of dirt on one cheek and a huge tear on the side of her plain green dress. But there was something interesting in her face. Maybe it was her eyes, for they were a rather peculiar shade of amber and gold. Or maybe it was the cocky way she tilted her head and blatantly stared.

"Father said you were coming," she blurted out, winning the attention of Kefthar and my father. Both of them immediately went down on one knee like they were proposing to the odd, skinny girl.

My father's hand tugged violently at my shirt and almost sent me tumbling. I managed to recover my balance, but not before I'd gone down on both knees.

"Rise," the girl said. "You know I don't like all that stuff. It's silly."

If my father was a Baron, and he was kneeling to this waif of a girl, did that mean that she . . ."

My father bolted up. "Benjamin."

I lurched to my feet and waited for him to explain.

"I'd like to introduce the King's younger daughter, Sepia."

I forgot about being suave, sophisticated, and or gallant. I'm sorry to say, my mouth dropped halfway down my chest, my eyes popped out of my head, and, worst of all, I gasped, *"She's* a princess?"

My father was probably wishing at the moment that I'd either never traveled into his dimension or else was hoping I'd suddenly be jerked out of it, yet he didn't say anything — at least not to me.

"Your Highness, may we have the pleasure of accompanying you to your father's banquet room?"

For a tomboy, which she was obviously, I had to admit, the girl, I mean the princess, handled his courtly gesture with much more grace than I'd just demonstrated. She walked over to my father, held out a velvet-green ribbon that she pulled out of her pocket, flipped the other end toward him, and gave him a rather nice smile.

Kefthar took a moment to glance back at me. Then he chuckled. As my father and Sepia (Wasn't that the color brown?) started walking down the gray stone path, Kefthar fell in behind, leaving me in the hexagon, staring at the guard with his wiggling-armed octopus. I sighed, shook my head at how strange everything was, and scurried after them.

Chapter Twenty-One

We were apparently walking in the more widely used section of the castle. The gray stone walkway turned into soft, fuzzy lime-green moss. I reached down to touch it, gaining one of those looks from my father and a giggle from Sepia. I soon discovered why. The phosphorous substance that had been providing our light as we walked was abundant in the moss, and it came off on my fingers. I started to rub my hands on my clothes, but Kefthar interfered.

"Here," he said, offering me a cloth.

I nodded my thanks, took the felt-like blue cloth, and rubbed. Amazingly, by the time I'd almost wiped all the glimmer off, Kefthar's cloth began to tingle and glow.

"Drop it," Kefthar ordered so brusquely that I did so without thinking.

My father and Sepia continued on. Kefthar and I were still lagging, but leaving behind trash in the castle couldn't be a good thing. I questioned it.

The big blue friend of my father's glanced down at me and smiled slightly with green-hued teeth.

"The cloth will not remain there long. Vegetation will quickly absorb it."

As if realizing that he'd sounded overly gruff, Kefthar suddenly clapped me on the back hard enough to make me wince. "It is good that you ponder. A warrior must always consider such things. Leaving traces of one's presence is dangerous."

He'd misunderstood my thinking, but I nodded. Whatever our miscommunication, I certainly didn't want him to clap me on the back again.

Meanwhile, we caught up with the others. My father glanced back at me. "It would be wise to be cautious, my son. Some things here are not what they seem. *Flither* is not exactly dangerous to our kind, but you'd probably prefer not to have your skin turn green."

"Yes, thanks for the warning, Dad. Kefthar thankfully saved me from that."

Sepia was giggling again. Her attitude was another irritation.

"Hey, I don't live here, remember?" I snapped.

"Benjamin, you must address her as *Your Highness* or *Princess Sepia*. She . . ."

"Please stop that. His attitude is refreshing. No one ever bothers to shout at me like that. It might even be good for me."

My father didn't reply. He merely turned around and resumed walking. This time, Sepia didn't join him. Instead, she took a step toward me and offered me her strip of cloth. Then she smiled broadly.

The kid was all of twelve. She had very little going for her in the way of looks, even if she was a real princess, but I decided that I should be nicer. I picked up my end and held it stiffly.

"What is the purpose of this?" I asked. "Does this keep you from getting cooties or something?"

Sepia laughed. "What are cooties? How do I get them?"

She didn't understand how strange this fabric connector was. I could see that.

"Forget it. Why don't you just hold both ends of the fabric?"

Sepia stopped, turned, and stared at me. "I have honored you by offering you the other end. Don't you know that?"

I laughed. Sepia hadn't taken back her fabric. It was still dangling from her outstretched hand. I caught it up again, not really wanting it but figuring it must be a big deal for her. Then I shook my head.

"You're absolutely right, Sepia. I didn't know that. In fact, I don't know anything about this place. That's the problem. My parents just pulled me into it, and now there are blue-skinned guards attacking me, castles that go on forever, and . . ."

I swallowed the words I'd been about to speak. Princesses with red hair and freckles might not be the right person to complain to. I decided I'd better be a little more cautious about what I said to her or to anyone in this world. My father was right. I was ignorant about the place I'd been dropped into.

"That is *zaplitty*," she said. "I knew you were different. We're going to be friends. Okay?"

She was as ugly as a speckled toad, but I liked the way she'd stood up to my father. I nodded, smiling. "Okay, Sepia. Why not. Let's be friends."

If only I'd known how dangerous that statement was! But despite my decision to be cautious, I'd just plunged into another great crevice, one that brought me perilously close to . . .

The King is around the next bend, Garland suddenly roared, scaring me half to death. *Be sure you hit your forehead with your fist and then collapse onto the floor.*

I was just about to ask about the collapsing part when about a hundred blue guards, dangling from overhead, lowered themselves down to the ground and surrounded us. I dropped the bit of cloth I'd been holding and screamed out, "Garland! We're being attacked!"

Yes, I know that was a stupid thing to do. I realized it later, but I'd never lived anywhere where huge, three-limbed, cross-eyed, blue-skinned aliens with noses like miniature cornucopias dropped out of the sky. Maybe if I'd been in this other world longer or if . . .

But, anyway, that's why Garland, suddenly and all at once, having entered straight through layers and layers of heavy stone, descended on the scene. Oh, I don't mean she crashed a hole in the walls. She didn't do that. She just kind of winked herself instantaneously right into the middle of the King's grand entrance chamber, and I'm afraid that because of the way I'd sounded when I called out in panic, she was spitting mad!

Upon seeing a fire-breathing dragon in their midst, most of the guards retreated immediately skyward. The twenty blues on the ground who were surrounding the King, backed up without thinking, leaving him totally exposed to the danger. The King's face turned the same color as a fire hydrant, and I'm absolutely positive the look in his eyes wasn't from being happy to meet me.

And I? What was I doing during this major disaster of dynamic proportions? Well, due to my lack of training in *handling unusual alien situations*, I'm afraid that I was rather unqualified to handle any of it. In other words, I backed up against a wall, shut my eyes, and began murmuring, "There's no place like home. There's no place like home!"

Chapter Twenty-Two

I'm even more ashamed to admit that it was Sepia who called a halt to the whole nightmare. She apparently inhaled a vast quantity of air and expelled it at top volume, yelling, "Enough. Everybody freeze!"

And they did — more or less. Even Garland. The dragon alit on the soft green moss, the guards all stopped screaming, and the King took a couple of steps backward while glaring angrily at his guards and at everyone else in general. Even my father and Kefthar turned to stare at Sepia.

"Why is there a dragon in the castle?" Sepia asked.

"Yes, why is there a dragon in *my* castle?" the King echoed with a slight deviation about whose castle it was.

Garland turned her rotating eyes in my direction, which caused everybody else to turn THEIR eyes in my direction, and the result of that is that I died right there on the spot.

Well, not exactly. I just wanted to very badly.

"Who are you?" the King demanded.

"I'm Benjamin," I said rather weakly (after an extremely intense moment of silence in which I silently prayed that my mother would whisk me instantly out of the castle and back home.)

My father stepped forward then, proving once again that he was a very brave man. "This is my son, Lord Benjamin," he told the King. Then, just at the point when I was sure my father would launch into a brilliant excuse for my behavior or at least give the most eloquent apology for my stupidity, he didn't say another word. He simply crossed his arms and stood looking at me, his face expressionless.

"I see," the King bellowed. "Then would you explain, Lord Benjamin, just exactly what this dragon is doing inside my castle?"

There was nothing to do then but confess the whole story. (What was it exactly?)

I took a deep breath, pushed my shoulders back (before my father could once again order me to do so), and said, "Well, you see, Sir . . ."

"You must address the King as "Your Majesty, Benjamin," my father interrupted.

I nodded. "Your Majesty . . ."

"Benjamin has agreed to be my friend, Father," Sepia blurted out.

The noise level in the room when Garland had flown in, belching fire at various walls and chairs, had been several decibels above pleasant to listen to, but when Sepia said that about my being her friend, the volume roared to almost twice as loud.

"What!" yelled the king.

"You did what?" roared my father.

Every guard in the whole room erupted into low-pitched rumbles of dismay. Even Garland let out a "whifffff," lifted her head, and swung it from side to side. Her eyes began rolling about like two cherries in a revolving bowl.

In fact, the only people in the whole room who weren't upset with me at the moment were Kefthar, whose body was jerking with chuckles, and Sepia, who was grinning back at him.

There was no point in attempting an explanation then. I waited, watched, and wondered just exactly what I'd done wrong.

Eventually, Sepia quieted everyone down again. (I did have to admire the girl for her gumption, even though she'd been the cause of finding myself in boiling water.)

Anyway, shortly after that, the guards lowered back down to the moss flooring. The King marched over and stared down his rather large and dill pickle-shaped nose at me, and Garland's eyes stilled. I began to breathe again. In fact, I started to hyperventilate, noting the King's expression.

"Father, it is too late to intimidate Benjamin," Little Freckle Face said. "He has already accepted his role. Besides, as I was telling you . . ."

"Yes, I know," the King murmured, sighing heavily as he looked at his daughter. "You fooled this poor newcomer into pledging to you. I should be angrier with you than with him . . . except . . . Oh, rutabaga! Let's get back to the former matter of the dragon. What is a dragon doing in my castle?"

At that instant, the King was looking at Garland and not glaring at me. I attempted to quiet my breathing, calm my racing heart, and find the place where my brain had gone into hiding.

"Uh . . ." I said most eloquently. "Uh, Garland kind of crashed the party because . . ."

"Who is Garland?" the King demanded, looking about the chamber for an unidentified person.

"The dragon, Father," Sepia interrupted.

"Oh," said the King. "How do you do, Dragon Garland?"

Garland nodded, making it look as if she were offering her respect.

"Go on, Lord Benjamin, although I do not believe Dragon Garland crashed anything."

"Yes, Your Majesty. What I meant was that Garland flew through the walls into this room because I got — well, I guess you could say — nervous when your guards dropped down from the ceiling. I'm not used to that sort of thing, you see."

"So you called the dragon to your defense? Duly noted. But what connection is there between you and this dragon? Are you a dragon rider, then, Lord Benjamin?"

I glanced at my father, wondering if he wanted to take over. His face was still void of expression. He was offering no encouragement, but, on the other hand, he wasn't lecturing me or interrupting to correct my speech. I sighed and looked away.

Kefthar and Sepia were still grinning at me. I swallowed, sighed again, and tried to answer the King's question.

"I think so, Your Majesty. Garland seems to have adopted me for some reason."

Because you're cute, Garland told me, hopefully sending the message only to me.

"I see," said the King, stroking his rather immense white-gray beard. "I shall have to think about this mess.

"Dragon, now that you see that your dragon rider is well, would you be so good as to remove yourself from my castle?"

Everyone's eyes moved from me to the dragon. That was like having fifty pounds of chains taken off my back. I sighed, relieved to be no longer the main focus.

Tell him I am sorry to have disturbed his day. I shall wait for you outside unless you have further need of me, Benjie. Garland informed me.

She didn't wait for my response. She winked out before even hearing my question about what it meant to be friends with a princess.

I can always hear your thoughts, Benjie. As for your question, that is easy. A friend is a friend. It means the same as in your kingdom. However, everyone gasped at Sepia's announcement because of the prophecy. It says that . . .

"Lord Benjamin, you will sit at my side during our feast so we can talk. Sepia, you will, today, sit on my other side. I wish to hear more from you about this friendship. A lot more," the King demanded, eyeing me as if he were still debating whether he should feed me or throw me into the dungeon.

I bowed my head. I wasn't sure if I should thank him for the honor or not. He wasn't exactly inviting me to dinner. He was commanding my presence. Did that require an RSVP?

"Come," the king ordered, then motioned to Sepia. As she approached, I was struck again by how young she was. The girl had just stopped a semi-riot, ordered about a hundred guards, and argued with her father. She was amazing. But what was the prophecy about her? Why was it unwise to be her friend?

I was just about to ask Garland to repeat the information about the prophecy when the King asked me a question. It took all my concentration to respond to him, and I worried that I'd still get it wrong. That was the first of many questions. The King suddenly launched into his own private grilling, apparently wanting to know exactly who I was.

In the middle of my explanation about the education I had gotten at Pinecrest Academy, the King turned and started walking further down the green moss path. I finished my sentence and glanced behind us, wanting to go rejoin my father, but then the King asked another question and after that, another. I had no choice, therefore, but to continue at his side. Behind us, marching two-by-two, the guards and my father and Kefthar all followed, silent except for the tread of about a hundred men marching in step.

Throughout the interrogation, Sepia remained at her father's side. I suppose she could hear my responses, but she kept interrupting so frequently I wondered if she even listened. Meanwhile, her input only sank me further in the eyes of the King. I could tell he didn't like her friendliness towards me.

The way ahead was becoming more elaborate and ornate. Heavy tapestries hung on the walls. Most of them held scenes of flowers and trees and maidens playing with large-sized balls, but one or two of them showed men fighting with swords and spears. I observed several with dragons in them. But not one of the dragons looked like Garland or her friends. The tapestry dragons possessed fiercer eyes and claws that looked ready to rend and kill.

I wanted to ask about the depictions, puzzled by the discrepancy with what Garland had told me about dragons, but the King didn't give me any opportunity to ask anything. He was still prying into my background. And Sepia was still continuing to butt in, taking up every moment of any potential silence.

The seemingly endless path we'd been following for what felt like miles suddenly opened up into a cavernous hall that looked exactly like the pictures I'd seen in books of ancient, ornate palaces. Heavy brass sconces, alighted with giant candles, welcomed us into its depths.

I stopped and looked about for someplace to sit. A meal would be nice, too, I thought, as my stomach began to growl. Unfortunately, we hadn't come to the end of our trek. The King veered sharply to the right. I started to do the same, but a great roar issued from one of the men behind us, and I turned. The blues were breaking formation and spreading out, fanning across the chamber's entrance and its walls. The King paid little attention to their maneuvers. He continued walking, pausing only to raise one eyebrow and say, "Hurry, boy."

I scurried to catch up. Jogging back to his side for some reason gave Sepia the idea of handing me her ribbon again. I certainly didn't want the silly thing. I wanted to pretend to ignore her offering, but the King was eyeing me strangely again. I took the ribbon's end from Sepia's outstretched hand and bowed my head as I'd seen my father do.

Apparently, that was the right thing to do. The King nodded approval and then resumed his march at an even faster clip. Sepia, catching my eye with a wave from her other hand, winked at me.

She was just a kid. I didn't want her flirting with me if that's what she was doing, and I started to tell her so, but the King asked another of his many questions.

There was no doubt we were deep inside the inner sanctum by that time. Blue-skinned servants scurried here and there carrying loads of sheets or tablecloths and house items of the sort that one doesn't discuss. (Okay, chamber pots. Happy?)

The palace or castle — whatever it was — had taken on an atmosphere of wealth. Elegance was obviously its interior decorator, although, for me, it felt overdone. Draperies of rich dark velvet in gold, turquoise, and scarlet were arranged like ocean waves across the walls and ceilings. Sconces filled with lit candles made their dangling diamond baubles glitter and dance in rainbows of illumination. And the furniture, heavy wooden pieces that looked impossible to move about, were all cushioned in fabrics of satin and velvet — material that was obviously made for a King.

The chambers we passed through were each as different as the one before, displaying patterns of color, unique objects that I wanted to stop and look at, and, disgustingly, stuffed wild animals whose eyes looked beady and vacuous from death. I was getting bored from the richness of the assault. It all seemed tedious with sameness.

And then, we came to a chamber with a golden staircase that climbed toward a star-filled sky. The stair's handrails and the vertical supports that serpentined it shone with a radiance that almost hurt the eye. The King began his tread upward. I lingered a second, running my hand on the heavy banister, amazed at the warmth of its touch.

"You must not anger my father," Sepia warned. "He is very hungry now."

I nodded and stepped onto the lowest step. The texture of it was like that of the earlier green moss. Except this growth was peacock blue and softer than the other had been. Nor did it have the same phosphorus quality, but then the room wasn't as dark, so I couldn't be positive.

There must have been sixty or more steps on the stairway. When we finally reached the top, I was winded, but not so the King or his daughter. They continued on with great speed. I glanced back. Our followers had thinned out so that only my father, Kefthar, and about ten of the guards were still accompanying us. No wonder it had grown quieter than before.

"We are almost there now," Sepia told me, winking again.

"Stop that," I hissed at her, huffing from the climb and grouchy from hunger. I completely forgot about using her title or treating her as anything but some neighborhood kid who had latched onto me. "Don't get me into trouble again," I warned her.

Her eyes grew large. They even, for a moment, started to tear, but then she snorted a laugh. The sudden noise brought the King's attention back to me. Once again, his eyes were glaring.

Chapter Twenty-Three

The dining chamber, as they called it, was situated at the top right of the grand staircase. In appearance, it was just another of the many vast and elegantly decorated rooms, except for this one had a most interesting feature — an elongated wooden table that was spread with a bounteous feast.

Eagerly, I sat in the appointed chair and waited to observe protocol, but my mouth was watering. The smells were overpowering. My stomach gurgled and hissed from lack of sustenance, and the sight and odor of so many delicacies was making me almost ill from anticipation.

The King was seated beside me, Sepia on his other side of him, and my father and Kefthar across from us, when the most beautiful young woman I'd ever seen came walking into the room, accompanied by her mother. I had no eyes for the latter. The sight of the beautiful girl absorbed my vision. No words could describe the King's other daughter, but I shall try.

Her hair, long and tousled with curls, poured down her back in an ecstasy of auburn and gold. The candles on the walls set off shimmers in it that danced with each step she took. The richness of its glow took my breath away. And then she looked up. My heart stopped beating; my lungs no longer functioned. I drowned in her eyes — eyes of emeralds, of jade, of springtime. Her dark lashes were long and curled upward, her cheeks like the sunrise, her tiny nose — an enchanted flower.

I sighed heavily and long. Love strikes with such pain and sweetness. I wanted to fall at her feet, to kiss her sandaled and beautifully formed toes, to touch the ground where she walked. I wanted to . . .

Then the King smote my pleasure with the cruelest of words. "This is my older daughter, Saffron, betrothed to Prince Selmar from Tourset. And my lovely wife, Queen Marisa.

"My dear ones, this is Lord Benjamin, the son of our Baron and Baroness. You remember, Wife — Adam Thorne from *There*."

I could see the Queen now since I'd been severed from my heart's desire. She was old, probably about my mom's age, but still beautiful. Yet I could barely look at her. She was too much like her daughter, the wondrous Saffron. The betrothed Saffron. I sighed again, even longer than before, and grew even sadder.

Sepia tossed a biscuit at me. It hit me on my right cheek.

"Sepia! Shame on you, child. That was totally uncalled for. Apologize at once," exclaimed her mother.

Sepia stared down at her empty plate. I wondered where she'd gotten the biscuit. I wondered if I could eat it.

"Well, he doesn't have to fall in love with Saffron. Everyone else does, but he's my friend, not hers. It just isn't fair!"

"Enough," the King bellowed, shaking his head but laughing at his younger daughter's outpouring. "Let us eat."

A second ago, I'd been ready to, but with Sepia's words, my face turned tomato-like. Everyone saw that I'd fallen for Saffron? Was I that obvious? Had I embarrassed myself in front of them?

I sat, staring down at my empty plate. The servers were coming closer. They had first taken care of the royalty, but they were approaching me next. It didn't matter; I knew I'd be unable to swallow a bite. Even the piece of biscuit I'd slipped into my mouth lay there like a stone, refusing to go down my throat.

I took a gulp of the water in my goblet, but it wasn't water. It was some kind of bitter root tea. I choked, dropped the rest of my biscuit, and began to cough.

"Oh, dear," the Queen cried out. "Are you all right, Benjamin?"

I could barely breathe. Tears rolled down my face, but I bravely waved my hand in an effort to assure them I was fine.

Do you need me? Garland yelled into my mind.

I shook my head before I realized that he wouldn't be able to see that. *Don't come. Please. I'm dining with the King and his family. Don't come here,* I sent.

"You are being rude, Benjamin," my father barked out at me. "Answer the Queen immediately."

Had I missed something? Had I not heard a question? Everyone was staring at me. "I'm sorry. Did you say something? My dragon was speaking to me. She thought I needed help. I was just . . . ."

"Dragon? You're a dragon rider?" said the goddess of beauty as she turned her large, heavenly eyes in my direction, staring into my soul.

"I -- I -- I . . . "

"We saw the dragon, Saffron. She came into the castle, right through the walls, and . . ."

"Sepia, let Benjamin tell it. Do not interrupt people, my dear."

The King laughed. "Was she interrupting? He wasn't saying much."

That made everyone chuckle. Even my father. But Sepia didn't. She was staring at me, a curious look on her face.

"I'm sorry, Benjamin," she said. "Tell us about your dragon, PLEASE."

And so I began. I told how I'd first met Garland, how she'd followed me back to the house in my own world. I spoke of being carried in her claws and how I'd learned to ride on her back, about the warmth of her breath, the kindness in her voice, how I'd discovered that she could talk with me and I could answer her without speaking a word. Then I told them about the meeting on the road with the entire Weyr of Dragons. And they all listened.

In the past, whenever I'd tried to speak, no one had bothered to listen. I wasn't a good speaker; I'd been told that over and over. I bored people. But not this time. Even my father was intent on my tale about Garland. . . Even my father.

After the dinner: a scrumptious meal of biscuits, cornbread, fifteen kinds of vegetables, meat pies, fruit pies, casseroles of potatoes and eggs, platters of fresh fruits — some of which I'd never seen before — and desserts too numerous to count, we stood up and waddled off to another room. There, the servants brought us plates full of tiny pastries, decorated candies, and dried fruits with nuts, coconut, or chocolate over the top. I patted my stomach and shook my head. I didn't have one inch of room left, even though I'm sure it would have been delicious.

Sepia passed them up, too, but her sister didn't. My lovely Saffron gobbled up the sugary items like a harvesting machine. I wondered how long her beautiful figure would stay so perfect.

A servant brought us coffee. We had a choice of dark and thick or dark and thick, apparently in a variety of flavors. I passed on the coffee, but everyone else enjoyed their small cups of mud. Kefthar had three cups of it.

"Tell me more about your dragon," Saffron said, plopping herself down beside me on the couch-like seat where I was resting my weary bones. (Yes, I was exhausted! You would have been worn out, too, despite what you're thinking. I mean, imagine what the day had held — two different worlds, dragon riding and dining with a King and his family. Not your average day! My eyes were already sagging, and my body felt like I'd been in the washing machine on that final cycle where the water all gets squeezed out.)

Still, I had enough energy to be aware that Saffron's proximity made me very nervous. What if the King thought . . .

Forget the King's anger. It was Sepia who threw a dried apricot at me. I ignored her temper and turned to look at the beautiful Saffron.

"What would you like to know?" I asked her.

She crammed another candy in her mouth, chewed, and spoke without swallowing. "What does a dragon say?"

"Stuff," I said, trying not to notice that candy drool was running down the princess' chin.

"How exciting!" she gushed. "A real dragon. I'd be scared. I'd probably faint. I'd never even look at it. I'd probably drop down in a real faint."

"You said that," I commented without thinking.

I like the younger princess. She's a brave little one and smart, too. This one would make me yawn.

Garland, I can't talk with you while I'm trying to make conversation with the princess. The dragon just laughed, but I'm pretty sure she didn't stop listening. I felt her in my mind.

I won't go into details about the ensuing conversation I had with Saffron. As Garland had noted, the King's older daughter didn't have a spark of Sepia's intelligence. Only the latter's occasional shot of a dried apricot or prune hitting my chest or head with a thump kept me awake.

When a servant took me up to my room for the night, I was more than ready. My eyes observed the roaring fire under the stone mantel, the bathtub in a dark corner, and then the large, fur-covered bed. I ignored everything else, dismissed the blue servant, threw back the covers, and slid in. I think that even before my head actually hit the big, fluffy pillow, I had fallen into a deep and wonderful sleep.

Chapter Twenty-Four

The alarm sounded especially harsh that morning. My hand almost knocked the clock to the floor before I realized the importance of the day. I sat up and looked about me, expecting to see the raging fire, the stone mantel, the bathtub in the corner. But of course, I was back home again in my own bedroom.

I brushed my teeth, showered, dressed in my father's suit, and tried to refit myself to this environment. The shift was not easy. I kept seeing Sepia and her sister, the King and his wife. And Garland.

I am here, she said. *The neighbor's cat hissed at me. A dog being walked by its owner barked at me, and the paperboy rode his bike over my tail. I much prefer my world to this one. Can't we go home now?*

As I conversed with Garland, explaining that this was the world that I belonged to and intended to stay in, I made myself some coffee, put bread in the toaster, and boiled a couple of eggs. I was just sitting down to eat my breakfast when Harry knocked at the door. I let him in, poured him some coffee, and offered to fix him breakfast. He looked at mine and laughed.

"I've eaten already. Listen," he said, glancing down at his watch. "I know this is your first day of work. At first, I figured when you didn't call me that you'd arranged for a taxi to pick you up. Then I started thinking about it, and I knew you wouldn't do that. You're planning on riding your dad's bike all the way into the city, aren't you?"

I nodded, washed down my mouthful of toast, and said, "Yeah, it will be good exercise, right?"

Harry shook his head. "That road's not safe for biking, and it's too far for you to go. You're not a long distance biker. And look at the way you're dressed. You can't ride a bike in a suit. Do you know how sweaty you'd get? It's just not going to work."

He had a point there about the sweat, but I couldn't rely on neighbors to do everything for me. I had to grow up sometime. Why not today? I started to expound on that with Harry, but he wasn't finished talking.

"Besides, Benjamin, your father would never have allowed it . . .

That thought reminded me of a particular conversation I'd had with my father. Dad had forbidden me to ride his bike to work this morning, but that was just a dream, wasn't it? Besides, if he really cared, he wouldn't have left me. He and Mom would still be here.

". . . and Martha and I don't want you to do it, either, Benjamin. It's just too risky. Please, let me drive you there and pick you up. I have nothing planned, anyway. I'm just an old man. You'd be doing me a favor — giving me something to do. What do you say?"

I cracked my second egg, rolled it back and forth, and nodded. "All right, Harry. I don't know what to say. This isn't going to work every day, but I'm happy to accept your offer this morning. Thank you. I appreciate it."

Harry sat back in his chair then and took a couple of sips of the coffee. "Benjamin, I love you like my own son, but you make horrible coffee. Can I please throw this out and start again?"

I sighed and set down my mug. He was right. Whatever the secret for making good coffee, I didn't have it. The stuff I fixed never compared to his. I stood up and watched as Harry poured the full pot down the sink. Then, I paid attention as he went through the steps. Measurement seemed to be the key. Harry used only about half the coffee I'd put in. I scribbled down the quantity and taped it to the backside of the cupboard.

Since I wasn't riding the bike to work, I had a couple of hours to kill. Harry and I sat down at the table and discussed the mystery of my parent's disappearance. That's when Harry told me he had a new idea. What if I contacted the insurance company and told them that my parents were dead, and I wanted to collect the insurance? Wouldn't that make the company scramble to find the answers? They wouldn't want to pay my claim, so they'd be determined to find my parents — even more so than the detective.

It was a great idea. Leaving Harry at the table to sip his new and improved coffee, I went in search of the documents I'd need. I found all the information in my mother's file cabinet. Then I sat down in her chair and started calling.

By the time I was finished, my head was throbbing. I bent over the desk and massaged the pain.

It was Garland's fault. She kept chattering the same thing over and over. *But your parents aren't dead, Benjie. And you know exactly where they are. Why waste your time? What does this bring you?*

I was back in the sane world. I wanted Garland out of my head. But how did one do that? Should I make an appointment to see a doctor? A psychiatrist?

I sneezed. Feathers were drifting down out of the air. I started collecting them, catching them as they fell. Then I stopped and looked up; the flow was speeding up faster than I could handle it. Stop it, Garland. Stop it! I cried out.

I am real, Benjie. Do not doubt me.

"You okay, Benjamin?" Harry called out.

"Yeah, I'm coming. I just finished. I left messages, of course," I yelled out as I shut the door to my parent's office. "No one was in their office at this hour of the morning, but it's a start. They can check out the situation while I'm at work."

You cannot shut me out. I am your reminder of the other world.

"Want me to do anything?" Harry asked, refilling my mug as I sat down.

Your mother is crying. She misses you. Garland intruded.

I sighed. That was a cruel thing to say.

"You're already doing too much. Thank you," I answered Harry.

My mother left me. She didn't have to. I almost shouted into Garland's mind.

"This is tough on you. I can see it in your eyes," Harry said with a worried voice. "Are you sure you're okay to go to work today?" he added, laying his hand on my shoulder. His gesture (and Garland's words) were making my eyes swim.

She didn't leave voluntarily, Benjie. Neither of them did. Didn't your parents tell you that?

"The office could do without you another week, Benjamin. You don't have to rush into this."

"No, Harry. I need to do it. I mean, I want to. It's a great opportunity."

Go away! I'm trying to make a life here, I screamed at Garland.

Your life is in other world, as you call it. That is the place you belong. With your parents. With Sepia.

That did it. I was feeling pulled by two worlds until Garland said the name *Sepia*. Once more, I resolved to shut out Garland's voice.

"I'm starting Chatsworth in September, Harry. I really need to work first and raise a few bucks on my own. You know what I mean? I'll be fine."

Your parents need you.

I'd been gritting my teeth as it was, attempting not to respond to Garland, but her words were more than I could ignore.

Need me? My parents have never needed me. I'm not sure they even wanted me . . .

Harry was stirring his coffee round and round. I was positive the sugar had blended long ago. Was he doubting my sanity, too? Is that what he was thinking?

You're so wrong, Benjie. Your parents love you. They...

Harry was still staring down at his coffee, the spoon swirling the coffee in circles of black.

"Harry, I'll be fine," I repeated.

He chuckled and then picked up the mug. "I'm glad to hear that, Benjamin. Here's to you," he said, holding the mug in position for a toast.

I raised mine and touched my mug to his.

Then he smiled. "You got guts, Benjamin, and that's important in life. I know you're gonna make it, kiddo. You're a champ. Now, bottoms up for a good first day at your new job."

Chapter Twenty-Five

If only Harry had seen me in the real world, I doubt he would have had that much confidence. My first day was a complete disaster. I spilled coffee on one of the attorney's papers, broke the copy machine, tripped over a trash bucket, which spilled pencil shavings all over the beige carpeting, and temporarily lost an important paper that I was supposed to take from one attorney to another. And if all that wasn't bad enough, I stuttered every time someone spoke to me.

I was expecting to be fired at the end of my first day. I think it was only because of my parents' disappearance that I was saved from that. But pity can only go so far. Tomorrow, I knew I must do better.

Harry picked me up at 5:00. I was a sagging balloon by then, emptied of enthusiasm, self-worth, and energy. I dropped into the front seat and wilted even further, barely able to keep the stinging tears I felt in the back of my eyes from flowing down my cheeks.

Harry didn't say a word about my attitude. He drove down the road talking about a blue jay who'd spent the day tormenting the neighbor's cat. Then, when we were almost at my house, he pulled into his driveway and said, "I want you to come inside, Benjamin. We have something for you."

If I'd had a choice, I would have refused. I wanted nothing more than to lick my wounds in privacy. But Harry had driven me to work and picked me up afterward and been wonderful about my bad humor. I could do nothing else but agree to his request. I climbed out of the car and followed him into his house.

"There you are!" Martha cried out, happy, as always, to see me.

I hugged her and kissed her dry-as-leather cheek. She turned me around and led me into her warm, comfortable kitchen.

"Now, you sit down there," she ordered. "I've made a nice chocolate cake, and we shall celebrate you. . ."

I am sure she was about to say my first day of work, but she must have caught the look on either my face or Harry's.

"We're going to celebrate this beautiful day," she finished her sentence.

I gave her a quick half-smile and sat down, picking up a fork in eagerness. Already, the smell of chocolate was in the air. My mouth could almost taste it.

Harry had poured me a full glass of milk, and they even had a bowl full of barbecued potato chips in the center of the table. Neither of them could eat such things. I knew I was being honored. Barbecue chips and chocolate cake with a glass of milk were personal favorites of mine.

I tasted the huge slice Martha put in front of me and sighed with pleasure. Then I finished the rest, drank the milk, nibbled on the chips, and, in general, basked in the sunshine of Martha and Harry's love. It didn't heal the wounds of my horrid day, but it helped. By the time I trudged off home, I was feeling almost human again.

They are good people, Garland said suddenly, scaring me half out of my pants when I jumped.

"Don't do that. Make some kind of noise before you speak or something," I protested. My yell had startled the neighbor's cat. She let an indignant meow of protest before fleeing off to hide inside another bush. Poor thing. First the blue jay and now me.

You would not like me to become visible here. Nor, I think, would you appreciate my blowing on the back of your neck first. That might upset you more than a voice in your mind.

Garland had a good point. Yet I hated to agree with her about anything. I continued walking, hoping I wouldn't forget to mind speak and frighten any other wandering pets.

Isn't someone missing you in the other world? I asked.

Garland chuckled. I am too young for a mate if that is what you mean. I am at the age of fostering.

I didn't bother asking for details about what fostering meant. Hadn't my day already been bad enough without a dragon following me home and talking nonsense into my brain?

At home, the first thing I checked was the answering machine. No calls.

I changed clothes and went out to look at the garden. The tomato and zucchini plants were like little slot machines giving simultaneous, winning payoffs. I collected basketfuls of vegetables and then attacked the weeds, watered, and did some snipping here and there.

For dinner, I chopped up a couple of the zucchini and tomatoes and plopped them into a skillet. I opened my mother's drawer of spices and read the labels, but nothing looked familiar. I shut the drawer and just used salt and pepper.

The phone rang, and I grabbed it. The cleaning lady wanted to know if she should come to the house. Knowing she had a house key, I told her to come whenever she wanted. She requested that I leave a check on the kitchen table, but I couldn't write checks. I offered to put cash in an envelope.

"That will be fine," the woman said, and we disconnected.

I discovered that even a short phone conversation like that one could destroy an entire meal. Dinner was burnt and tasteless. I ate it anyway.

When I woke in the morning, the first thing I thought of was that I hadn't dreamed. I whistled in the shower that morning and smiled as I dressed.

For breakfast, I ate boxed cereal, using the last of the milk. Another problem flashed its greedy eyes in my direction. I shrugged. Those kinds of problems were at least easily rectified.

When Harry arrived that morning, he honked his horn. I ran out to the car and invited him in for coffee, promising that it was a good brew that morning. He chuckled but still shook his head.

"Don't forget to lock the door, Benjamin. I've already had my coffee," he added. "Oh, and be sure to turn off the coffee machine."

After doing those things, I climbed into the car and buckled in.

It's a nice day in both worlds this morning, Garland informed me.

I nodded in agreement.

Harry backed out of the driveway and headed down the road. It became obvious that he'd already had a full measure of coffee. He was full of good humor and even told me some amazing jokes on the way to the office. He had me really cracking up by the time we arrived. It was a good feeling to laugh that hard and definitely a great way to start the day.

Maybe it was the jokes, or maybe my bad luck from the day before had been depleted. Either way, my second day on the job went much better. No klutz, no falls, no stutters.

It was payday, too. I didn't get a check, of course, but it was something to look forward to. I watched the faces of the others as they opened up their envelopes. They were quick about it, sliding the checks into their purses or their briefcases after a brief look to see that everything was okay. There was a different feel about the place after that. It was as if the sun had suddenly won through the clouds.

In the evening, when Harry picked me up, he didn't have to provide the cheer. I was feeling good.

At my request, we stopped off at the grocery store and picked up some things. I grabbed two gallons of milk, three boxes of cereal, and some TV dinners. Then I added the non-essentials, filling my cart with things that might come in handy — one of them was a small book entitled *Quick and Easy Dinners*.

I offered to treat Harry to an ice cream cone, but he said he needed to get back home. He looked a little worried but, when questioned, said it was nothing, that Martha was fine.

When he pulled into my driveway, I insisted that Harry let me go get the basket of tomatoes and zucchini I'd picked. I laughed, telling him about my dinner the night before — the burned dinner.

"Oregano," he said. "That's what I like to spice things up with," Harry was back to being his usual self. The twinkle in his eyes had returned. I supposed then that I'd only imagined his worry.

And so the days slid by, and my first weekend alone came and went. I spent most of Saturday gardening and then cooked dinner for Martha and Harry. The meal was eatable, believe it or not, but I could see I needed to keep working on my cooking. While I'd been preparing one thing, everything else had gotten cold.

The following week, I talked with the detective twice. Still no answers. I spoke with the life insurance adjustors. Until there was proof of the death of my parents, no money was owed to me. The auto insurance company said my father's car had been totaled. A check was in the mail, but until further notice, all auto insurance had been canceled.

I continued my hoeing and weeding, working out in the vegetable garden until I dropped at night from fatigue. I even bought some marigolds and pansies for the front yard.

When darkness fell, I watched TV and pretty much attempted to go through the motions of being normal. Yet all the time, Garland continued to speak into my mind, chatting amiably, complaining about my world, and entreating me to go back to the other kingdom.

After becoming adjusted to my routine, I was almost ready to go back for a visit, but the truth is I didn't know how. Each time I lay down on my bed, I wondered if I'd see my mother and father that night. But I didn't make the transfer. I remained in my world, dreaming normal dreams until . . .

Chapter Twenty-Six

I went to bed late on that Friday night; I'd stayed up watching a horror flick, a laughable one, which was the only kind of horror I'd watch. Still, the monster attacked me in my dreams. His fangs had somehow grown several inches and were dripping with someone's blood. I was armed with only a rather large-size English textbook and held it up in front of me like it was the cross people use for protection against vampires. The alien monster wasn't impressed. His fangs lowered down, his saliva dripped onto my face, and I screamed.

The scream woke me. I was lying in a green meadow. Garland was looking down at me, a worried expression in her open-wide eyes with the pupils revolving like cat-chased rats in a circular maze.

"I have called for Sepia," Garland told me. "She will know what to do."

"You what?" I cried out, sitting up with a lurch. "I don't need a twelve-year-old brat telling me not . . . ."

"Brat?" I heard the familiar voice.

I turned to apologize, but my mouth slammed shut, and my eyes bulged. It was Sepia, but not Sepia. Her hair had lightened. It wasn't carrot anymore, and it hung loose, forming curls that writhed with light and shine. But that wasn't all. Instead of the twelve-year-old she'd been the last time I saw her, Sepia looked at least fourteen. She had, well . . . she'd grown in certain places that were most becoming to a young lady. In fact, she was halfway beautiful.

"What happened to you?" I blurted out, too mystified by the situation to recall that I was supposed to be addressing her with the formality of her position.

She laughed. "You mean, what didn't happen to you?"

Garland and she thought that was hilarious. Sepia giggled saucily while the dragon roared with laughter, and I, the one left out of the joke, had no idea what they were talking about.

"What do you mean — what didn't happen to me?" I asked, sighing and giving in to their laughter with an odd chuckle of my own.

"You didn't age. That's what. You're exactly the same as before."

"Don't be silly," I laughed. "I saw you just two weeks ago!"

Garland and she exchanged glances. I felt uneasy. When had they had time to form such a friendship? Why was Sepia so changed?

"It has been over two years since you were here, Benjamin. More like two and a half, really. My sister is married now. I know that will sadden you, but she is content. She lives far away, though. I miss her sometimes."

"Wait. You're telling me that two weeks in my world took two years in yours?"

Sepia didn't answer, but she turned to face Garland. "Could that be true?"

Garland's eyes stopped rotating. She was calm, smiling even. "Time between the worlds is inconsistent. I have noticed that in my travels."

"Are my parents okay?" I demanded suddenly.

I could see the King's castle in the distance. That meant that we were far away from my parents' castle. I panicked when Garland didn't answer me right off.

"Your father is fine, but your mother is having a difficult time. She carries this child late in her life."

"What?" I'd been looking out across the fields, taking in the scenery. With Garland's words, I swung around to stare at her. "My mother is pregnant? No! She couldn't be."

That set Sepia off into another round of giggles. "You're so funny, Benjamin. Why couldn't she be? She's married to your father, isn't she?"

"What's that supposed to mean?" I demanded, whirling around to glare at Sepia. "What are you suggesting?"

Unlike the Sepia of two years ago, this one seemed more cautious. Noting the fierceness of my expression, she took a step backward.

Nothing she'd said could have calmed me more quickly. I swallowed my instant of fury and drew breath. "Sorry. I just . . ."

Sepia nodded, but she didn't step close again. She reached out and stroked Garland, scratching at her chin. "I only meant that your father is quite handsome, Benjamin. I didn't mean any insult."

"I'm sorry. That wasn't like me."

I'd been a grump, but it was just because I was worried. I wanted to explain that, but I didn't want to take the time to do so.

"Please, Garland, please could you fly me to my parents? I need to see my mother."

My dragon didn't speak. She crouched for me to climb, which I did at once. Then I looked down and saw Sepia, all teary-eyed and alone and miles from her castle.

"What are you doing out here, anyway? How did you get here?" I yelled down at her as I looked about for her horse.

"I rode," she answered calmly. The guards and the horses are back behind that cluster of trees," she said, pointing to a small wood over to the right. "The guards are rather afraid of your dragon and prefer not to come closer."

"Okay. That's good. Okay, to leave you then? You'll be taken care of?" I asked, considerably relieved.

She sighed. Then her eyes flashed with the former temperament I'd grown to expect from her. "I do not need you to watch over me, Benjamin. If you wish to leave, then do so."

There was something in her tone that puzzled me, but I didn't have time to work it out. I needed to see my mother.

"Good. Let's go, Garland," I ordered, and the dragon immediately lifted up and soared over the field.

When I looked down, Sepia was still standing in the same place. She didn't wave to me or call out. Her shoulders looked lower, her head bowed, and her wondrous hair had fallen around her face. I wished she'd look up. I wanted her to do so. But she didn't.

As Garland's feathered wings flapped us away, I thought about how much Sepia had changed. She'd become almost pretty. That hair of hers, sparkling in the sun. Her nose was so demure. She was still saucy and bright. I liked that about her. I always had.

I closed my eyes and thought about the way she'd looked in her yellow dress. Sepia. No wonder they'd called her that. She was autumn. Not brown, as I'd first thought, but the color of leaves, oranges, golds, copper.

I recalled green eyes, but they might have been her sister's. What color were Sepia's eyes? I wondered about that as Garland carried me toward my parents' castle. I really couldn't remember. I wished I'd looked. I'd wished I had taken a moment and . . . Darn it. What color had Sepia's eyes been? For some reason, it seemed very important to know. Why did it matter?

When we reached the castle, the bridge across the moat was down, and people were crossing, going freely in and out of the inner courtyard. I marveled at that, wondering what the purpose of a moat was if it was always this easy to cross.

The people, seeing Garland, scattered to the sides. Some of them even ran back across the bridge, returning, I suppose, to their houses. But there was nothing I could do. I rode Garland down to the ground, thanked her, and jogged off toward the inner chambers.

My feet were loud against the wooden flooring. They pounded as if I were much heavier than normal. No, more like as if they were echoing across a chasm.

Guards stopped me before the entrance to my parents' hall. "Halt," they demanded, raising spears that were sharply pointed and aimed at my chest.

Blue skinned warriors with gourd noses. I remembered the one in the king's palace who had challenged me and then prostrated himself. I wondered what had happened to him.

This time, I wasn't afraid. I met the man's eyes and equaled his gaze.

"I want to see my parents," I told the man whose sword point touched my breast. "I am Lord Benjamin."

The man's sword did not lower. His eyes showed no recognition.

"Let him go," said a voice I recognized, as Kefthar stepped forward.

The blue one's sword dropped. I spun around and clasped Kefthar's hand. A moment passed with his hand in mine. Our handshake was firm and strong.

"Welcome back," he greeted me. "Your parents will be delighted to see you."

Kefthar spoke to the guards in an alien tongue, then led me further into the inner chambers of the castle. I was grateful. It wouldn't have taken me long to get lost inside. I scarcely remembered the route.

As we walked down long, decorated halls, I sort of recalled various tapestries and ornamentations. Everything did seem familiar, but I knew I couldn't have retraced my way to my mother's room. Had I even been there? I wrinkled my brow, trying to remember.

I found my mother sitting in a small sitting room that was located next to her bedroom chamber. She was reclining in a plump, comfortable-looking chair, her feet on its fat, pillowed footstool. Ladies-in-waiting or friends, I couldn't tell the difference, were sitting beside her, keeping her company. The women were all working on small hand sewing or stitchery projects.

Kefthar stopped at the door to announce me: "Your son has arrived, Madame."

"Benjamin!" my mother cried out. "You came back!" She had a moment of awkwardness trying to rise. I didn't know if I should offer assistance. But two of the ladies came to her side. They heaved her to her feet.

Tears were streaming down my mother's cheeks as she came toward me. My mouth dropped. I looked down, not able to meet her eyes. When had she started caring so much for me? I had never seen her cry.

A stab of guilt punched me in the stomach. I should have come before now. I should have been by her side, but it wasn't my fault I hadn't returned sooner — not exactly.

I kissed my mother's cheek and hugged her gently. The fragrance of her had changed. She smelled of lilacs and roses, a pleasant smell but one I'd never associated with her before.

Our hug was very difficult. The baby protruded, making me not only uncomfortable, but worried that I might hurt the baby somehow. When Mother moved back, I tried not to stare at the mountain between us.

But, it seemed that my mother wanted me to see the bulge. She even took my hand and placed it on her swelling. "Don't you want to feel the baby kick?" she asked.

Not really. I wanted my mother back, slim and normal. But of course, I didn't say that. I left my hand where she placed it, feeling clumsy and tongue-tied. Yet when the baby kicked, and I felt it, I was awed. There was a child in there. A baby. Wow!

I met her eyes, and then I, too, smiled. "When?" I asked, my voice so high and screechy I could barely recognize it. "When will it come out?"

To me, it looked like I should be having a brother or sister immediately. Like at that very moment, in fact.

As if she'd read my thoughts, my mother laughed. "In a few weeks," she said. "A baby comes on its own schedule. We must all just wait with patience and faith."

The bit about faith was rather jarring. She'd never spoken the word, to my knowledge. Yet, I held back, not wishing to question her about changes in her philosophy. One thing at a time.

"And is it a boy or a girl?" I wanted to know.

Mother shrugged and smiled more deeply. Her eyes sparkled as if I'd amused her. I suppose I had. I seemed to amuse a lot of people in this other world.

I was examining her face, adding to stored memories. If I'd done a comparison between who she used to be and who she was in this land of dragons and dreams, perhaps I'd scarcely have recognized my hyperactive attorney mother. Her face seemed plumper, definitely younger than when I'd last seen her. She was more beautiful, too, more beautiful than ever, even though the midsection of her normally shapely body was badly distorted by my new brother or sister. But there was something even more obvious — a difference in her bearing and her nature that was new and so startling I could hardly believe it. She was still inside . . . and peaceful.

I remembered all the times I'd tried to talk with my mother, and her eyes had flitted about, eyeing the case she was working on, the pattern on a desk blotter, the dust on a corner of her shelf. She'd never stopped thinking about things. Never been motionless. She'd never once looked deeply into my eyes, not like she was doing at that moment.

As if she read my thoughts, she placed her hand on my face and caressed my cheek. I swallowed hard. My legs felt weak.

My mother took her other hand and held my head. Then she brought me closer and examined me even more thoroughly.

"You are so unchanged," she said. "Are you still only seventeen?"

I nodded. Of course, I was. Only a few weeks had passed since graduation. How could I have aged? Yet Sepia had. She'd blossomed. Her body had filled out. I stopped that thought cold as I remembered that I was standing in front of my mother.

I shook my head. "Time doesn't pass as quickly back home. I haven't aged — well, maybe a week's worth."

My mother's eyes teared freshly. She bit her lip. "Has it been too awful for you?" she whispered.

I didn't know how to answer that. Did she want the truthful version?

I suppose she saw what I didn't say in the depths of my eyes, for she suddenly dropped her hold on me and turned away.

When she looked up again, she finally noticed that the women were all staring. Mother blushed. Then, with a wave of her hand, she indicated that it was time for them to leave.

I closed my gaping mouth and watched as, without a word, each lady rose, bowed to my mother and to me, and departed through the room's entry, carrying their bundles of stitchery projects and their purses of thread and sewing supplies. The scent of their passing reminded me of my hospital stay. Whole bouquets of flowers rustled by me in pinks, blues, and creams of satins, velvets, and assorted cloths of elegance and refinement. Flashing eyes, pretty eyes, eyes that called and beckoned. Oh, and smiles, too. Once more, my legs quivered, but this time with the desire to follow the ladies of my mother's sewing group.

As if again she could read my thoughts, my mother caught my hand, took it in hers, and led me away from the distraction of being close to so many beautiful women.

"Sit down, Benjamin. Let me look at you. Are you well? Are you okay?"

My eyes escaped and flitted to the door, but the ladies had all sallied forth, as a professor at my school used to put it.

I sighed. "I'm fine, Mother. I have missed you, though. I tried to return, but I could not. Each night, I lay on my bed and tried to imagine myself back here, but it never worked. I couldn't make myself dream."

"Benjamin! Son! You have returned to us," my father cried from the doorway.

I stood up and went to him, unsure whether to expect him to hug me as my mother had done or to offer up a hand for him to shake. He didn't notice my hesitancy. He threw his arms around me and pulled me close, squeezing me with such a fierce bear hug I worried for my ribs.

No need. In another second, he'd already pushed me away and stood, holding me at arm's length. "But you are so little changed," he roared as he peered into my eyes. "What is this? Have you not aged at all? You're not even growing chin hair yet."

Deflated as always in my dad's presence, I stared down at the floor.

"He says it has only been two weeks, Adam," my mother said from her comfortable chair.

"Two weeks?" My father newly examined my face and body. "Amazing," he thundered out. "I do not understand how this whole thing works. That is for sure. Your mother is younger than she used to be. I feel the strength of my youth tenfold. Yet, you are still as unchanged as if time had stopped its flow."

"Sit down, Benjamin," he ordered, turning to glance at my mother. "Are you all right, my love?"

She blushed, nodded, and then sighed. Then she reached up to smooth down her hair as if hugging me might have disarranged it.

My father's eyes softened. His voice, when he next spoke, no longer thundered. "So, Benjamin, have you made any decisions? Is this a permanent stay or another short one?" he asked, turning to examine me again.

"It's just a visit," I said. "I wanted to see if you were both okay. Then I heard about Mother. Are you truly well?" I asked, wondering again how she was doing.

She smiled. "Oh!" she cried out suddenly. "The baby is kicking. It's so much stronger than Charlotte's kicks. I'm positive this one's a boy."

My father laughed buoyantly, but I frowned over what she'd just said. Who was Charlotte? As if I'd asked the question aloud, a knock sounded, and a nurse, receiving permission with a nod from my father, carried in a small toddler wearing a frilly yellow dress. The child had ringlets of curly, blonde hair. Her cheeks were chubby and pink. She had my mother's eyes.

"This is your sister, Charlotte," my mother told me, her face aglow with love.

"But w..w..where did she c..c..come from?" I stuttered.

My father laughed. My mother smiled sweetly. "I'm sure your education has been thorough in such things, Benjamin."

Catching my eyes and seeing the heat on my face, she changed the subject. Laughingly, she added, "It is true that Charlotte was rather a surprise for us. A pleasant surprise, of course. I was carrying her when you were here last, Benjamin, although I didn't know it at the time."

The nurse set the child on the ground. She was walking already. She ran to my father, who lifted her up and set her on his knee.

"Then this is the second baby," I said, indicating my mother's stomach.

Dad laughed. "Our son seems deficient in arithmetic," he kidded me while he jiggled the child up and down on his knee. "How did you earn all those "A's" on your report card if you can't do basic math?"

"Math?" I echoed. His jump from subject to subject, as usual, confused me. I glanced at my mother for clarification.

"He means that you were our first child, Benjamin, so it follows that the child in my womb is our third, not our second."

My face flooded with heat. A moment before, it had felt brown-toast warm. With my mother's explanation, my face flared into baked Alaska. The word my mother had used, *womb*, was something we kids had only whispered. I'd never heard anyone say it out loud.

Charlotte was tugging at my father's shirt. "Down," she said. "Down." He lowered her to the floor, and she ran to her mother's side. "Mommy, Mommy," she cried as she flung herself into my mother's arms. Luckily, my mother was expecting it and knew just how to restrain the little imp. Charlotte still got her exuberant hug and kiss.

"How is my sweet one?" my mother murmured into the child's ear.

This scene made me very uncomfortable. It was as if dropping into a fantasy world hadn't been quite enough. Someone in charge had just tilted the cameras and turned everything upside down. The same parents I'd known all my life, the ones who hadn't wanted more children, were all of a sudden producing babies with the contentment of newlyweds. They were acting like a family. It was madness. Screaming insanity.

But just then, little Charlotte wiggled out of my mother's arms and waddled over to stand and stare up at me.

She was shy. Her eyes didn't quite meet mine, but I could tell that she wanted to. She bobbed and twisted, her little body awkward and yet amazingly cute. She was twisting her long velvet dress with one hand and giving me flirtatious little girl smiles.

"Hi," I said, not knowing what else to do.

"Hi," she answered back. She stood a moment more, rocking back and forth, eyeing me more confidently. Then, she seemed to make a decision. She handed me her rag doll.

I turned it over and examined it.

"Pretty," I whispered. "Is it yours?"

She nodded and giggled. I handed the doll back, and she took it and hugged it close. "Doll," she said. "Mine."

I nodded. I looked over at my mother, needing a little help with the conversation, but Mom wasn't saying anything. She was smiling at my father.

"Does it have a name?"

"No," she told me, her mouth pursed in thought. Then her eyes flitted to my face again, and she smiled.

"Doll," she said.

I doubted she'd be able to answer any of the questions that plagued me about this other world. She didn't seem to have much of a repertoire of words.

"Charlotte," I said, trying to come up with something entertaining. "That's a pretty name. Is that your name?" I asked stupidly for want of anything else.

It appeased her, however. She smiled, dimpling again. "Charlotte," she repeated, pointing a fat finger at herself. "Benjie," she continued, pointing to me.

So, she knew my name. The fact gave me pleasure. I smiled, then glanced at my parents.

"We've shown your picture to her almost every day. She knows you're her brother," my mother said.

"Wow! So, the next time I come for a visit, you're gonna have five or six more brothers and sisters for me to talk to, right?" I asked, whistling in wonder.

"No," my mother said abruptly. "This is my last."

The look she gave my father then wasn't quite as loving as usual. Poor Mom. She must really be feeling ill to look at him like that.

Chapter Twenty-Seven

I spent the rest of the day with my parents and sister. It went amazingly well. They were changing in this alternate world, suddenly becoming the parents I'd always wished for. Why had the transformation occurred so late? Why had they needed to leave me to discover they loved me? I wanted to ask them, but such questions were not easy to speak when years of silence had been the pattern. We were strangers still.

Dad and I went for a ride later. He put me on a green horse — one hardly through basic training, testing me to see if I could handle her. Luckily, horseback riding was one of the things for which I had some talent. The skittish mare wasn't even a challenge. I could read Dad's face that I'd amazed him. For the first time, he couldn't find anything to criticize.

After the ride, Mother and I had more time to talk. She told me about the accident. I was all ears. It was what I'd been wanting to hear Since the first time I'd arrived in what I finally learned was called Wizardland.

She was sitting in her red comfortable chair, as she called it, the one with the little foot she couldn't find a position that gave her any ease. Beside her on a small table was a drink, which she sipped now and then. A small plate of finger foods sat beside it, but she didn't nibble any. I'd never seen her eat between meals. She'd always kept herself busy with the hankies she used to embroider initials on.

There was no sewing in her lap while I sat with her that day. Instead, her fingers clasped each other or remained limply on the baby that kicked abundantly and, according to the expression on my mother's face, sometimes painfully.

I took up a position in a straight chair, one with a dragon tapestry at the back and a war scene on the seat. Sitting on top of the battle scene, the shifty-eyed ogre and six knights laden with metal armory fought while I watched my mother's face as she finally told me what had happened the day she and Dad disappeared.

"We were on our way to see you graduate, Benjamin. We were looking forward to it and eager to see you. Having you home, having you live with us, that was something we'd dreamed about. We wanted it."

Mom smiled sweetly while I struggled valiantly not to allow my face to reflect my disbelief. Let her think I accepted her words. I supposed that she needed to remember things differently, needed to believe that she and Dad were looking forward to having me at home.

I must have been convincing. She continued, laying it on even more thickly. "Your father couldn't wait to introduce you at the office. He'd been bragging about what a good student you were, how honest, how dependable. We were so proud of you, Benjamin. You do know that, don't you? We're so very proud of you."

I nodded, although it was a bit of a surprise to hear. They'd certainly never said anything about being proud before. I wondered if this was more of the fantasy she kept weaving into her story.

"Adam was driving. It was such a beautiful day. I was embroidering, of course, and Adam had started whistling a song they were playing on the radio. What was that song? Let me think. Oh, I don't remember now. It will come to me later.

"Anyway, that's when a tire blew. That had never happened to us before. I still can't understand how it did. Our Beamers always have the best of care. We get a new one every six months. You know that.

I don't know why the Beamer let us down. It was supposed to be known for its reliability. And all four tires were new.

"But when the tire blew, Adam swerved. We almost hit a truck. I remember that. Then, suddenly, we weren't inside our car. We were standing on a hill nearby, watching the road with our Beamer and that truck frozen, both of them as still as a couple of concrete buildings.

"Adam was angry about the situation. He ranted at the injustice of it, the being delayed from our trip part, but I knew right off that what was happening to us was not something minor, not just an obstacle that might make us late. I don't mean that being late to your graduation was minor, Benjamin. I mean . . ."

"I know, Mom. I know what you mean."

She reached over and patted my hand. "I know you understand, Benjamin. You're always like that. Easy going. Adaptable. I told Adam that. I told him you'd be good at this."

"But I was telling you the story. Let me get back to that.

"Something was extremely wrong, and it was obvious. We'd been moved magically from the inside of our car to the top of a hill. I tried to make your father see that, make him understand that ranting about our dealership and the mechanics wasn't going to help."

"But your father was in full pitch, roaring for the judge and jury. Only there wasn't any way to prepare for a trial. It just happened, or it would have happened — our instant death, except the King's magician had been traveling in our world, looking for something, he told us. We never knew what it was. All magicians are secretive, you know.

"He walked toward us and stopped Adam in the middle of a tirade. The magician just clicked his fingers and froze your father into some kind of listening mode. Mercy, I'd like to have that ability."

Her eyes pondered that for a bit. Wisely, I kept still. In a moment, she returned to her story and went on.

"The magician gave us a choice — death or coming here. It wasn't much of a choice, Benjamin. Either way, we lost you. But Adam and I thought that between two evils, coming here was the lesser.

"Benjamin, you have to understand that no matter what we'd decided, we didn't have an option to go to your graduation. We couldn't say, "Let's wait until Sunday to journey to Wizardland. It was an instant decision, yes or no, and we took it. We took it because we didn't have a choice.

"I'm not sorry we did, except for leaving you all alone, but as I've told you, there was nothing we could do about that. It wasn't until we met the King that we found out we could do any bargaining at all. Then your dad haggled hard and strong. He got us this castle and the title. In this kingdom, you're nothing without a title. But he also negotiated for something else, Benjamin, for you.

"The King, in exchange for certain legal documents drawn up by your father, agreed to let us have the opportunity to win you over. You are free, Benjamin, free to come here. Free to remain in the world you grew up in, in the place you know.

"I'm sure we've made it clear what we want. We want to be a family. A real family, this time, Benjamin. Would you give us that chance? Please agree to stay here."

I closed my eyes and then opened them to stare out through her open window. Her room overlooked a field; whether it was a pasture or a wild meadow, I couldn't tell, but I could smell the clover and the honeysuckle that twined up the castle wall. I could breathe in the sweet fragrance of roses, the old-fashioned kind that scented the air. I could hear birds singing, insects humming — all the sounds of nature.

I sighed and looked down. "Mother, you ask too much of me. I want to be with you and Father, but to leave everything behind? You wouldn't have done it, not if you'd had a choice. Remember? You were an attorney, a well-respected one. You know what it feels like to earn the respect of people, to do work that means something. I want that, too.

"So far, I've never had that opportunity. I start Chatsworth University in September, but even now, I have a job — for the first time, Mom. How could I give that up to go back in time just so I can live in the Renaissance? In this world, you don't even have computers. You don't have electricity. How can you endure that?

"So, did you tell him?" my father asked, stamping into the room with such a heavy tread it was as if he were one of the knights in the tapestry I was sitting on. I glanced at him to see if he wore full armor or at least a chest of metal. He didn't, but his arms glistened with sweat, and his muscles bulged and glowed slightly red. He didn't look like an attorney.

Mother shifted again, then groaned slightly. I stood, wanting to help, but I didn't know how to offer assistance or what I could do to ease her load.

My father strode forward and took her hand. The exchange of their glances did more than I could have. Her cheeks flushed. She sank back against the chair and sighed softly, contentedly.

I collapsed back into my chair, once more squishing the armored knights and the set-upon ogre.

"Yes, Adam. Benjamin was just saying we've gone back in time. Maybe we have, dear. I suppose he's correct, but we didn't have a choice. Benjamin still does. I don't think he wants to join us."

Tears were suddenly tumbling down her face, creating dark circles of moisture on her blue velvet dress.

"Mother, please," I said, standing up again.

"Garland is asking for you, Benjamin. Go see her. I'll stay with your mother. This isn't good for her. She should be resting."

I was relieved to be free of my mother's tears and the guilt I felt from them. I bolted from the room. But then I turned and watched as my father lifted up my mother and carried her to the bed.

What did Dad mean that this wasn't good for her? Was my mother's life in danger? Didn't they have decent doctors here? Who would be delivering the baby? What if something went wrong? No hospitals. No medications. No emergency facilities in case she needed something.

I was chewing the side of my mouth with worry by the time I made my way down the stairs and out into the courtyard where Garland waited.

"The King has commanded your presence," Garland said.

I backed away. "No. I can't leave. My mother isn't well."

"A command from the king must be obeyed," Garland said, her eyes flashing fire engine reds.

"But I can't just leave. I have to tell them, at least. . ."

"No. You do not wish to make the king unhappy with you," she told me as she kneeled down so I could climb up quickly.

I glanced back as I climbed her leg. Someone was carting a barrel of food or drink to the kitchen. I called out, "Tell my parents I've been called to the king's castle. I'll be back as soon as I can."

Chapter Twenty-Eight

It was cold in the sky. I shivered until Garland breathed his fiery breath back in my direction. It stank of spoiled meat, but it did ease the frigid nature of our flight.

Will I have to walk that whole way again? I asked, remembering the tiresome path that wove in and out and around about.

Garland chuckled. The king gave notice that his summons was urgent, so I shall fly you directly there. His entry hall will be large enough for my body, don't you think?

"Don't make him mad," I said, shivering with more than cold.

Garland didn't respond. We suddenly winked into darkness and came out in the middle of the king's grand entrance chamber. A journey that had taken an entire day before had just been completed in minutes. I opened my mouth and closed it. Was such a thing any more miraculous than waking up in an alternate world?

The giant blue guards rushed forward with spears taut. Garland let out a single flame. It singed one of the tapestries. A guard tore it off the wall, flapped the heavy wall-hanging onto its back, and smothered out the fire. The other guards all backed away, swords lowered, spears not as ready to aim at us. Garland shifted her head about, eyeing each of them. She didn't need to warn anyone twice.

Give them your name and tell them you are here at the king's command, Garland said as her huge head continued swaying back and forth, ready to flame again should the need arise.

My voice boomed out in full volume. I hardly stuttered at all — only once, on the word *king*.

Two guards took off running. I remained where I was, feeling much more confident than usual, probably having something to do with sitting atop a fire breathing dragon.

The chamber where we'd landed was icy cold. The guards probably didn't feel it. They were wearing armor, and besides, I thought that possibly their blue skin might be less conducive to heat loss. But I was shivering.

Garland breathed out several small puffs. It helped. My teeth stopped rattling.

Sepia was the first to arrive.

"Stand down," she ordered the guards, who were still standing at full charge with their spears ready for combat.

I don't think they liked taking orders from her, but they obeyed, if grudgingly — at least until the king arrived. Then, it was once more a full-battle-attack position.

"Stand down," the king roared. There was no dragging obedience that time. Immediately, the guards ran to their positions at the doors and walls, and their weapons remained lowered.

"Why have you brought your dragon into my palace?" the king roared again, this time eyeing me. "Dragons do not belong inside, Lord Benjamin. Didn't I make that clear to you last time?"

I wasn't cowered by someone merely yelling at me. Hadn't I spent a lifetime at the other end of wagging teacher fingers, snarling professors, and parents who'd always seemed disappointed by the things I'd accomplished?

I raised my chin and looked him in the eye. "Garland said you needed me at once. I didn't want to linger walking along your widening pathways. Isn't that right? Didn't you demand my presence immediately?"

The king seemed surprised by the tone of my response. His eyes narrowed in thought.

"Why did you order Benjamin here, Father? What's wrong?" Sepia asked, her eyes green as baby leaves.

I smiled down at her, enchanted by her cute, upturned nose. Such a pity the girl was so young. I was positive that Sepia was going to be far more beautiful than her sister.

The king ignored his daughter and growled out, "Well, all right. But get down and send your dragon away. I want no dragons in my palace."

"Father," Sepia prodded, tugging at his jacket.

The eyes that viewed her did not relent as I'd seen them do before. He remained stern as he glared at her. "Go away, daughter. This is between Benjamin and me."

Gasping, Sepia stared with wide eyes at her father.

"Now!" the king roared.

Sepia lifted up the sides of her dress and ran down the corridor that led to the left.

Meanwhile, I'd dismounted and sent Garland off to wait for me in the outer keep. I still had time to notice the shapely appearance of Sepia's ankles as she speedily retreated. Her light green dress clung modestly but quite appealingly.

Now then," said the king. "Come with me."

I followed behind him, as mystified as before. What on Earth could the king want from me? And why?

We walked for a space of time in silence, the king checking frequently that I was still keeping up. At last, we arrived at the chamber where he wished us to be. The king waved the guards away, shut the heavy brass doors himself, and gestured for me to sit.

"Now then," he said again when he'd pulled a chair closer so we were uncomfortably eye to eye. "We shall have us a little talk, won't we."

I remembered the chamber we were in. It was one I'd found immensely distasteful the visit before. Dead animals were arranged on shelves at eye height. Hanging on the walls were bodiless creatures draped from nails. Sad-eyed and dead, dead, dead. In fact, everywhere I looked, the glass beads of their soulless eyes peered down as if watching. The room made me feel ill.

"Uh, Your Majesty," I interrupted. "Could we p. .p. . possibly go s . . s . . somewhere else? The a . . animals . . and the st. . st. . stuffiness . . it m . . m . . makes me . . ."

"Good grief, you're green," said the King. He bolted up, threw open the doors, and tugged me out of the room. I shut my eyes for a moment, not caring where he took me, but I was relieved when I felt a cool breeze on my face. He'd led me to an outside garden. I breathed in and out.

"Thank you," I said. "I just c. . c. . can't stand. . ."

"All right. All right. Sit down."

The king's brow was creased with impatience. I knew the signs. My father frequently looked like that during his years of practicing law. He'd often shown that image when scolding me. I took a deep breath and waited to hear the lecture.

"You are not suitable as a king," Sepia's father said.

"What?" Had I heard wrong? "King?" I repeated.

"Exactly. Not my choice at all."

He stood up and paced a moment. I swallowed a couple of times and wondered what I'd done wrong this time. Was sanity finally sputtering its last gasp? Listening to the council of dragons, visiting an alternate world, hearing a king tell me I was not suitable to be a . . .

The king turned to look at me again. "Princess Sepia is the younger of the two. She is my royal heir."

I blinked. Otherworld was often confusing. In fact, it was almost always confusing, but this . . . this was even worse.

"I see you still do not understand our ways," the king said, sighing gravely. "That is another mark against you."

He took up his pacing once again. His feet would soon wear down the pattern on the elegant tiles. I wondered if the etched blue flowers were already a shade lighter.

"But," the king said. He stopped in front of me again to pierce me with his eyes. "But," he said, sighing heavily. "She has befriended you, so there is nothing I can do."

I wondered if he was pondering dungeon kinds of things. Would a beheading solve his problem? Without thought, my hand rose to massage my neck.

He cannot, Garland intruded. *He cannot do anything to harm you. The laws would not allow it. Neither would I.*

"And so, despite my distaste, I must accept this strange tide of events," the king growled, still glaring at me as if I'd just announced I had some horrible disease or something.

"Are you saying that p . . p. . p. . Princess Sepia and I are supposed to . . ."

I could have kicked myself for the stuttering. I'd stopped doing that years ago, but for some reason, since I'd started visiting Wizardland, the embarrassing habit was back in full force.

"It is a distinct possibility," he said, bowing his head. "The odds have increased by sevenfold with this latest return of yours. Thus, you are forewarned."

Forewarned? Did he mean there was some way around it? Or forewarned, like doom was approaching?

"I would prefer not to have had it occur, but . . . fate is fate," the king thundered, angry once again.

He built a fist of his hand and used it against the wall. It was a cement wall. I winced, feeling his pain.

"Thus, I bow to it. I hope you will do so, too?"

There was the punch line. (No pun intended.) Would I stay? Would I marry his younger daughter? A kid of what — fourteen?"

"Listen, Your Majesty. I'm not from here, and I don't p. . p. . plan on r. . r. . remaining here, so this f. . f. . fate you're talking about is not g. . going to happen."

I stood up and stepped backward since the king had just taken a step in my direction, his knotted fist still tight, and, although slightly red and bleeding, looking like it was ready to smash into my face.

"Besides, your daughter, Sepia, is only — what, f. . fourteen? You sh. . sh. . shouldn't even be thinking about b. . b. . betrothing her; I mean, that's just my opinion."

The king's face was growing as red as his fist. What if he were suddenly seized by a heart attack? Would it be my fault? Would I be tried before a panel of jurors or unceremoniously marched off to the next firing squad?

Still, I had to continue. I could see from his eyes, his glaring eyes, that he hadn't gotten my message yet.

"Let Sepia grow up f. . f. . first. She needs to be a k. . k. . kid for a while, and then . . ."

Perhaps I'd gone too far. The king reared back, and, I think, for a moment, almost did hit me. Instead, he took several deep breaths as he held his injured fist. Then he marched over to the wall and struck it again. I was very glad that he hadn't used his fist on me. This time his hand put a very deep indentation in the plaster.

"I was not asking for your advice, Lord Benjamin." The king ground out the words as if his teeth were grinding coffee beans. His eyes and voice felt cold as winter snow.

I nodded. Now was not a good time to argue. It was a really good time to take off. Unfortunately, I didn't have permission to do so yet, and my dragon was still somewhere outside.

Garland? Can you hear me? I mind-sent.

Either she ignored me, or she was too far away to hear. Her silence took away the last dregs of my courage.

"You are saying that you are not interested in my younger daughter?" the king delivered each word as if they were pellets he'd shot via slingshot. They stung, as did his spit, which was accumulating on my face. Did I dare wipe it off?

I was wishing heartily for my own slingshot. It had worked for David against the giant, Goliath. Maybe it would be applicable in my case. How had I fallen into this mess? It was insane. In my world, showing interest in a kid Sepia's age would get a seventeen year a one-way ticket to jail.

"Your Majesty," I began and then stopped, trying to unscatter my scattered wits. I took a couple of deep breaths and thought doubly hard.

"Oh, here you are," called out the queen as she entered into the secluded garden area where we'd been having our *discussion.*

I smiled at her, bowed my head, and prayed that the past conversation was suddenly and permanently concluded.

"You have come too early," the king said grouchily. "There has been no resolution. It seems that Lord Benjamin does not care for our daughter. Or else he is attempting to barter in a most unusual manner."

"Barter?" the queen cried out, examining me as if she thought I'd just sprouted horns.

Garland, where are you? I sent it again.

I'm sleeping. I'll converse later, she yawned rudely, and I think, she more or less hung up on me.

That interchange got me into still more trouble. The queen had apparently asked me something, and I hadn't heard. I explained that I'd just been speaking to my dragon.

"Oh, we quite understand," she said, waving one hand in the air as if swatting a fly. "A dragon rider is such a nice thing for a son-in-law to be," she informed me.

Inadvertently, I groaned — loudly. Then, as if things couldn't get any worse, Sepia jumped out of her hiding place and threw one of her shoes at me.

"You monster," she screamed. "How dare you turn my father down. It's not like I WANT to marry you. I'd rather die first. I'd rather marry a bill collector, or a tax man, or even a blue guard!"

Her mother gasped and turned pale.

The king put his hands to his head and shook it back and forth. "Life should not be this complicated," he said, groaning louder than I had. "Daughters shouldn't throw shoes. Sons-in-law should do as they are ordered. And dragons should never fly into castles! Do you hear me, everybody?"

He roared so loudly it's possible that people in *my* world heard him — even with headphones and music blaring out.

The queen, used to such outbursts, hardly even noticed the volume of it, but what she did suddenly observe was her husband's fist, which was steadily dripping drops of blood all over the stone pathway.

"How could you do that to my husband, you beast!" the queen cried out, glaring at me. "Guards! Guards!"

Get me out of here, Garland, please. Sepia's throwing shoes at me, the king is yelling loud enough to be heard on Pluto, and now the queen is about to have me arrested.

"Father, he is calling his dragon again," Sepia yelled, glowering.

I should have been angered by her betrayal. I should have hated her for all the trouble she'd caused me, but I couldn't. Sepia was, unfortunately, as cute as a junior high cheerleader. I stared into her angry emerald eyes, memorizing the moment. Then I turned and bolted for the door.

I almost made it, too, but the girl launched herself at my feet in a tackle that would have taken down the most swift and capable of all quarterbacks. I felt like a bulldozed tower.

"You're my friend," she yelled intimately into my ear. "You agreed to this."

I opened my mouth to argue about the meaning of the word "friend," and she pounced. Her lips met mine. For ten seconds, sweet music played.

"Ah," said the king. "The end of the lovers' spat."

I gasped and sputtered.

Sepia stood up, dusted off her green velvet gown, and extended a hand to jerk me up. I declined, jumped up, twisted around, and this time made it through the door, down the hall, through thirteen chambers, and out into the great hall before she could catch me. Then I threw myself up on Garland, and we took off, blinking through double stone walls and out into open space.

"Take me home, please, Garland. I don't mean where my parents are. I mean my home in my own world. This place is nuttier than a candy bar. I cannot take one single minute more!"

Garland turned her head to look at me, twisting her neck most impossibly, something that not only amazed me but worried me enormously since we were flying through clouds at a speed greater than most cars on the freeway.

"What about your parents?" she demanded. "Your mother is about to have a new baby. Any day now. You can't desert her!"

I shook my head and laughed. "Yeah, that's a good reason NOT to stay. Do you think it would be beneficial for her to watch her son be dragged off to the dungeon? Head removed. Body dissected limb by limb?"

Garland's head swiveled around, but not before I'd seen the flaming highlights of worry in her eyes. The pupils were doing the tango.

"I told you that I would not allow that."

Then she sighed, exactly like a person. A moan later, she added, "I shall return you. But I know you will ask me to fly you back here soon. It is your fate. And next time, you will . . ."

"Don't tell me! I don't want to know what you think is going to happen. I know. I'm never coming back. I've had it with this place. Fly me home, Garland. Please."

Chapter Twenty-Nine

Yes, I know I'm a coward. There were all kinds of reasons to stay — my parents, a new sister, and whatever the new baby — whatever gender it turned out to be. There was Sepia, too. That kiss she'd given me. It was a good kiss, one I'd like to explore. Except . . . I couldn't. That would be wrong. She was fourteen!

No. To return to that world would be like choosing to live in madness. First off, I didn't fit there. I was a high school graduate ready to go off to the University, just about to start my life in a place where BMWs raced on freeways and computers connected us to world news. We had microwave ovens and coffee pots that didn't rely on campfires, and, for heaven's sake, our toilets flushed. The fact that my parents were stuck in that situation was sad. But it didn't mean I had to be trapped in some loony bin of antiquity.

Of course, on the positive side, my parents were offering me a loving relationship, a real family, and a position. And then there was Garland, my dragon...

No, to think about that would put me on the path of psychosis. I had to get real here. I had to live in a world where magic was an illusionist's trick. A world where dreams didn't invade normality. A world where there were no dragons.

How boring. No dragons? Does that mean no unicorns or magicians, either? Garland was up early, pounding her thoughts into my head. Why wouldn't she let me alone?

I got up out of bed, poured my coffee, and took it out into the backyard. A mourning dove was cooing to his mate. His head bobbed when he saw me, but he didn't fly away. His lady love was sipping water from the cement pond, a small waterway Dad had set up that not only watered the vegetables but provided drinks for wildlife.

There were two redwood chairs under the grape arbor. To the left was a cement bench with entwined hearts on each side of the bench arms. Mom always laughed and said their concrete seat was the sort you'd see in a cemetery, but she smiled up at Dad whenever she said that, a smile that belied the teasing of her words, a smile that she wore whenever she looked at her beloved husband.

Over the years, my parents had worn one side of the bench smooth. It was the corner where they always sat. I'd seen them often, Dad's arm around Mom, both of them sitting so close together they could have invited the whole neighborhood to occupy the space beside them.

There was an engraving on the bench if you knew where to look. Down in the corner on the right side, it said:

When two hearts entwine,

it is forever.

All my love,

Adam

What was the girl's name I'd met the first time I dropped in on my parent's world? I drank half my coffee before I remembered. *Serena*. I could barely picture her now. I recalled no more than a fan teasing me. Sparkling eyes. A pleasing mouth.

Then there'd been Sepia's sister, Saffron, with her appetite for sweets. Would I have ever sensed what Mom and Dad felt for each other? With either of those girls? How often did a love like my parents' come around?

It would come with Sepia, Garland said. *The two of you fit. Your hearts would entwine forever.*

I finished my coffee without speaking. I was trying not to think about Sepia, trying not to remember the way her eyes had been so sad when I'd left her on the hill that day. The remembrance of it was a stake in my heart. She looked the same way when I'd run from her in the palace — maybe even more so. The pain had been deeper. The love she felt for me had almost pierced my heart.

She was just a kid, for heaven's sake. So she had a crush on me. What of it? She'd get over her feelings. Everyone did.

Except my parents never did. But that was different. They were adults. Except they hadn't been when they'd first met. They'd fallen in love during high school and then continued dating through their college years. All that time, they'd never looked away from their feelings, not once. Never cheated. Never strayed. Never for a moment stopped loving each other.

If Sepia were old enough, would I love her? If I spent more time with her, if I got to know her better . . . would it one day be for us like it was for my parents?

I shot a glance at my watch. Time was rolling by. I still needed to shower and get dressed before leaving for work.

I left the mourning doves cooing to each other. The lady dove was taking her morning bath while the male watched, protecting her, I supposed.

I walked through the backdoor, set my mug on the sink, and was just heading for my bedroom when the phone rang. Harry was on the other end.

"Benjamin, I need you. Come over, please. Can you do that for me? Can you meet me at the door, lad?"

I shot a glance at the clock, but it didn't matter what time it was. I was going. There couldn't be any other response. I didn't dare ask what was wrong. I suddenly knew this was about Martha.

I was right, of course. She'd died in the night. Harry had woken up beside her. He'd let her sleep in, but she hadn't been sleeping. She'd passed on, the sweetness of that smile of hers, as always, still on her face.

I didn't know what to say to Harry. I'd never had any experience dealing with grief. My parents' disappearance was the closest I'd ever come, but you couldn't grieve when you didn't know if they were dead. It was like twilight — neither dark nor light.

I sat with Harry while the paramedics came and carried Martha away. I was the one who thanked them and took down the information about where they were taking her. Harry, after letting me into the house, had just gone quiet, sitting in his easy chair, staring out the window as if the birds could explain to him why his beloved wife had left him.

After the ambulance departed, the house grew quiet. I called the office, explaining that I couldn't come in that day. I told them my grandmother had passed away. Then I fixed some coffee and returned to the sitting room, where I sat in silence next to Harry. The coffee I poured him sat on the coffee table beside him. It steamed for a while and then grew cold.

I got up a little later and asked Harry if he wanted some more coffee, but he shook his head. I saw that he was weeping and had been weeping silently. I hadn't seen many men cry like Harry did that day. He sobbed steadily as if he had a whole lake of tears inside him, like they were pouring out of him while his soul emptied. And when his tears were finally gone, he went right on weeping until his chest no longer heaved and his voice had grown stiff as a crackling leaf.

I tried to get him to eat some lunch. I brought in some canned soup, but Harry just shook his head. He wouldn't touch the food I brought him, not even the crackers I put in his hands. His head was bowed over. His body was shriveling as I watched. I wondered if I should call his doctor.

The afternoon dulled. A dark gray fog covered the ground. I threw the window open and allowed the chill of the air to descend across our sadness. One of the mourning doves perched in the tree outside. It cooed woefully as if it understood our grief. And then my tears began to fall, and I wept almost as heartfully and as copiously as Harry.

At last, when we were both shivering and Garland began scolding me, I shut the window, threw a blanket over Harry, who was limply sprawled in his recliner and tucked him in. I doubt he noticed. I sprawled on the couch across from him, too spent to cry anymore.

Why, Garland? Why did this happen? No one was more special than Martha. And now Harry, what will he do?

I couldn't see the dragon, but I knew she was there with me. I felt her touch, the warmth of her breath. Her tail knocked against my leg. *Life is sometimes shorter for some. It was even much shorter for your brother.*

I sat up. I looked out the window as if Garland were there. *What do you mean? What happened to my brother? What brother?*

But I knew. Just as I'd known with Martha, I felt it inside me, like a lump, a hardness that shouldn't be there. It was painful, and the ache dug in deeper and deeper.

My mother bore a son.

I remembered the way the baby had kicked so hard. He had seemed so healthy. Why had he died? What had happened? Then I

193

remembered the fact that my mother lived in a place with no hospitals, no surgery rooms, and no doctors.

Is my mother okay? Is she recovering from the loss?

No. Garland said. *She grieves. She grieves like your friend, Harry. And your father, he rides each day into exhaustion. They are not helping each other. He should be sitting with her, as you do with Harry. He should be holding her hand, fastened to her side.*

So, now I had a double load of grief, except one was real and the other imaginary. Or so I tried and tried to tell myself. And when I closed my eyes, I saw my mother, no longer spry and young, but with a white streak in her hair and eyes so sad that the sight of them made the thorns in my heart dig in deeper.

That night, I walked Harry to his room. I put him to bed like a child; then I tucked the covers around him tight. He turned to the pillow beside his, and he bawled openly and loudly as if he had not yet cried. Had I done what I could for him? Or should I have taken him to my house instead of remaining in his?

I slept on the couch that night, and in the morning, I peeked in on Harry. He was lying on his back, his mouth open, and his eyes gray as the fog outside the sitting room window. The breath had left him. He was cold.

I supposed I should have closed his eyes. Maybe I should have pulled the sheet up and over his head, but I didn't. I retreated from the room that Martha and he had slept in and called for another ambulance.

Chapter Thirty

The police came out to talk with me. They were there as the gurney took Harry away. I signed what I was told to sign, then, ignoring the questions of the officers, I stood up, walked into the kitchen, and began making coffee.

Two deaths — even of old people — coming that close together were suspicious, the cops said. I nodded and got out the milk to pour into the pitcher that Martha always kept for it. The sugar bowl was full. I set it on the table with spoons for each of us. Then, I set the mugs down and waited. The aroma of the coffee beans soon filled the air.

I'd made the coffee just as Harry did. Black and strong, as he used to put it. When I poured the brew, the others held back for a moment as if they suspected I was attempting to poison them. But as I drank mine, one by one, the three officers all picked up their mug and began to sip.

And then the questions came. With my head in my hands, tears running down my face, I explained about Harry and Martha.

"No, such thing as a broke heart," one of the policemen told me, angrily it seemed, as he scribbled down every word.

"Yes, there is," I said. "A broken heart takes the meaning from life, then the body slowly crumbles, disintegrates, folds in upon itself." I don't know where those words were coming from. I didn't stutter. I didn't stop to pick and choose. I just thought about Harry and Martha and my father and mother, and I knew.

"Without a heart, the body no longer feels. It doesn't matter if it continues on. Not if it's empty, does it?"

I saw the looks on their faces. One of them got up to use the phone. I suppose they'd gotten a preliminary report. Maybe they'd finished Martha's autopsy. Or maybe they'd just found out the special conditions behind my parents' disappearance.

The policeman, the one using Harry's phone instead of his own cell, was staring at me, staring at me as if I'd just confessed to murdering people.

But it didn't matter what they believed, what anyone believed. I'd learned things that day that I hadn't known before. I'd learned about entwined hearts and what happened when hearts broke.

I finished my coffee and stood up. "I need to call the office," I said.

The ears of the cops almost stood upright as I dialed and spoke. No doubt the cops scribbled down every word I said. I saw several of them writing.

"I'm not going to be able to return to work," I told Mr. Dougherty. "Things have changed. Thank you for the opportunity, but I'm afraid I can't go back."

The suspicion in the man's eyes grew darker, heavier. They thought I was guilty. They convicted me over coffee. I didn't care. Not anymore. I knew what I had to do next. It wasn't important whether I had running water, an electric coffee machine, or a BMW in the garage. Love was all that mattered, and dealing with entwined hearts.

I poured each of them another cup, but I didn't fill mine. "I need to go back to my house," I said. I need to change my clothes.

I thought they'd object, tell me they were taking me down to the station, but they didn't. They simply downed their coffee and followed me across the Gillicutty's driveway, through the hedge gate, and over to my house.

I hadn't locked the door. I opened it and left it that way. In the kitchen, I saw I'd forgotten to clean up. The coffee machine was still full of day-old coffee. I tossed out the grounds, washed the pot, and made some more. While doing so, I called Garland.

I am ready to go back, I said. *You were right. I belong there.*

It probably wouldn't have mattered if I took a shower or not, but for the last time, I used a good shampoo, hot water from a tank, and soap not made from lye. I scrubbed, then dressed in jeans.

When I returned to the kitchen, I saw that the men had helped themselves to some toast. When I was handed a slice all nicely buttered and shiny with marmalade, I didn't turn it down. I'd hardly eaten the day before. I devoured it and ate the toast that followed.

I made a final tour of the house. I wanted to bring something to my mother, but it was difficult to choose. At last, I remembered the plaque on the cement bench. That was perfect. With a screwdriver I found in the garage, I pried my father's love poem off the bench and slipped it into my pocket.

If I'd had the time, perhaps I would have taken other things — some pictures, a favorite book, the present my father had hidden in the safe for my mother. But I didn't think of those things, and for some reason, I feared time was running out.

I fled through the gate of the backyard. The policemen probably didn't know it opened since it was covered in honeysuckle. We rarely used it, but after I ripped out a handful of stubborn vines, it was still pliable, although squeaky.

I ran into the front yard, sensing that my dragon was near.

One of the officers must have looked out the window. He alerted the others, and they all came running out the front door, but it was too late then. Garland was already swooping down out of the sky; her claws extended and her wings at full breadth. I don't know what the police will write in their reports. Another mystery, another strange disappearance.

Garland alit in a distant meadow, one where only a few cows witnessed me climbing up her stout legs. Then my dragon took to the air and winked out. In the inhale of a breath, we were back in the long-tailed grasses near my parent's castle.

Sepia, as if she'd been expecting me, was waiting. She'd matured to the perfect age and was even more beautiful than I'd remembered. Her lips were part honey and part juicy, red strawberries. Her neck, which I kissed generously, smelled like spring apple blossoms.

"Will you marry me?" she asked, and of course, I said, "Yes." All my doubts had been tossed when I fully understood about entwined hearts. "I must go to my mother first," I told her. She laughed, but there was sadness in the depths of her eyes, and a certain redness that spoke of recently shed tears.

I took her hand, and we walked together. When we were almost at the bridge across the moat, my father arrived, dirty and disheveled and astride one of the blue horse-like beasts. He called out when he saw me, jumped down, hugged me tightly against his chest, and kissed me on the cheek. When he released me, I saw that his eyes were red rimmed. He was crying as openly and as copiously as Harry.

He greeted Sepia, bowing properly to her. I remembered that I'd forgotten to do so, but she hadn't objected.

"We must go to Mom," I said. "She needs us."

With one hand entwined with my bride-to-be and my other clasping my father's, we sped to the chamber where I'd last seen her. She was just as I'd imagined, grieving alone, tears dripping down the front of her dress, with a white streak running through her long, black locks.

"I have come home, Mother," I said. "I've returned this time for good."

Her eyes looked up, and she saw me. She smiled. Then, her eyes widened at the sight of my father. She cried out, "Adam," and flung her arms open for his embrace.

He went to her, carried her back to the chair, then on bended knee, he laid his head in her lap. I knew then that everything was going to be okay. They were together again.

I started to leave, but I remembered the gift I'd brought, the plaque from the heart bench.

"Mom, Dad, I never really knew how you felt about each other. In fact, I was jealous of it. But the truth is that I just didn't understand.

"Martha Gillicutty died, and Harry couldn't live without her. He passed on the very next day. He and I grieved together. Then, I think, he journeyed to Heaven to be at her side.

I understand now what you feel for each other. I feel that way about Sepia, and she for me." I drew the princess forward and kissed her cheek. Then, because that felt so good, I hugged her closer and gave her a tender but deeper kiss.

My parents laughed. And after that, their faces glowed with happiness.

I tore my eyes from Sepia's, something not at all easy to do because when love hits with that kind of depth, it pulls you under into another world. Into a oneness like Harry and Martha had shared. Or like my parents had always enjoyed.

Sepia and I would have lots of time to get to know each other and deepen our friendship, but we already knew our hearts. Strangely, she'd known as that funny little twelve year old tomboy. It had taken me longer. Males were slow, I'd been told. But eventually, we got there. We saw it in the end.

Sepia and I would have a long time to share warm kisses while snuggling in the flowered meadows of Wizardland. I kissed my finger and dabbed it on Sepia's adorable nose; then, I turned to face my parents. I'd stuffed the thing in my backpack so I could ride Garland. I pulled out the plaque and handed it to my mother.

"You need each other. I understand now," I told them. "And Dad," I said, meeting his eyes with the kind of intensity he used to fasten on me, "you should know that, too. Through grief or joy — whatever life brings you. It doesn't matter. Just like the world you exist in. It only matters that you're together. Love is what's essential. Always."

My eyes left my father's. I could see that he'd understood what I was saying. He picked up my mother's hand and kissed it.

"I'm sorry, Darling," he said. I should have been at your side. Forgive me, please."

Forgiveness was in her eyes, as was the love she felt for him. In fact, it was so obvious that once, I would have turned away, shunning the strength of this visible emotion. But I didn't feel that way anymore. I reveled in what they were displaying, for it meant that I, too, could have that strength of feeling. I could forge entwined hearts, just as they had.

Still, I needed one more thing to be said. I wanted to be sure that my mother didn't pine away and that she stayed with us despite her loss.

"Mother," I said, almost demandingly. "We are together now. We are all linked in the entwinement of hearts: you and Dad, my little sister, Charlotte, and now Sepia — and the king and queen since they are Sepia's family and so will soon be ours."

"And there will be others, too, one day," my blushing Sepia added, so I kissed her again because she was right that she and I would one day have children of our own.

My mother sighed, brushed away a tear, and nodded. "You are right. Thank you, I have mourned enough. It is time to move on."

Her sadness still lay in the depths of her eyes. It would take a long time to fade, but as Dad wiped another tear away and Sepia sniffled, Mom called for her maid and said it was time to cast off her mourning. It was time to celebrate that I had come home.

Later, after everything settled down, and the wedding plans and preparations began, (No, I can't tell you that the king acted real pleased to find out that I'd returned, but as he'd said before, he was resigned to his daughter's choice,) then in front of all the nobles of the land, the king dubbed me, Prince Benjamin. Everyone applauded, including my mother and father, who were arm in arm, as usual.

Weekly rounds of fancy balls followed, which meant lots of dressing up. I had to attend extra lessons in comportment, as well as lectures about how princes must act from tutors who frowned as often as the king did. But it was all worth it because at each ball or royal event, Princess Sepia smiled up at me, and her radiance took my breath away. And at those ceremonial shindigs, we usually danced. (Yes, I was given dance lessons and drilled in etiquette.) But when I was able to twirl the love of my life around and around and kiss her, despite the scowls of her father, it was all worth it.

In between the formality and ritual, Sepia and I sometimes flew on Garland. That was the best of all, for the dragon willingly carried us both, with Sepia sitting behind me, her head against my back, her body pressed close, and her arms wrapped tightly about me. Soldiers maintained surveillance from below, chaperoning, of course, but it was still a burst of freedom and sweetness because we were together.

In a month, perhaps the scowls will cease. That's when Sepia and I will be given the huge wedding that my mother and the queen are working so diligently on. And that will be followed by a honeymoon far away from Sepia's glowering father. I look forward to the latter.

Sepia says that one day, I'll have to sit on the old man's throne beside her, but neither of us is in a hurry for that to happen.

Meanwhile, I have a lot to do: getting to know my little sister, becoming reacquainted with my *new* parents, riding Garland about, being the best friend of my fiancé, and learning all I need to know about what it takes to live in this brand new kingdom.

But I know that this is the land where magic and love are entwined. And I am positive that Wizardland is the right place for me to be.

Don't be jealous if you're reading this book. Even if Wizardland, the Land of Dragons and Dreams, isn't offered to you as a choice, just remember: Love is what counts. Only Love, and you can find that wherever you plant your dreams.